First Degree Sins

I0678537

MIRIKA MAYO CORNELIUS

FIRST DEGREE SINS   MIRIKA MAYO CORNELIUS

First Degree Sins

ISBN: 0970851782

Copyright © March 2014, Mirika Mayo Cornelius
An Akirim Press publishing

FIRST DEGREE SINS   MIRIKA MAYO CORNELIUS

<u>Acknowledgements</u>

All glory, honor, praise and total worship to God Almighty, Jesus Christ and Holy Spirit for every single thing because without Him, I am nothing.

To my son, I love you. To my husband as well, I love you. My parents – you rock, I love you, and thanks for everything. Although gone from earth but always present and alive with the Lord, my granny Dora, I love you still. See you and the rest when I get there.

To my readers, thank you and I want you to enjoy this one as you have enjoyed the others. Thanks for your support.

More Akirim Press Books

Books by Mirika Mayo Cornelius

Secret

Colored Lily: Poppa Took My Innocence

Paton

Ain't Quite What I Thought!

Ain't Quite What I Thought! 2

Inside the Gates of Doons

Sunny Sides of My Shade

Murders at Gabriel's Trails: The Complete 5 Part Series plus bonus Sins of Bain

Books by Rod Cornelius

Diggin' Gold

The Trusted

Single Again

Ghetto Eyes

The Best Kept Secrets

Ugly

Books by Cyan Deane

Dead Man's Mayhem

Execution's Karma

Table of Contents

First Degree Sins

So what if they think I'm crazy. I'm the only one who knows the truth.

Chapter 1

As I place my groceries on the conveyor belt, she continues to stare at me with the side eye, barely able to concentrate, unknowingly only scanning one glass dish when I'd stacked two. The craziest thing is that she's looking at me like she thinks I'm the one who is out of my mind. She should ask herself that same thing. I certainly hope the store is getting this foolery all on camera because this bimbo is literally ringing my items like she's a ninety years old woman with a walker and two arthritic hands. Like I said, I'm not the one who's crazy.

Peering to my left side, the manager shoves a shopping cart into the lane I'm standing in and rushes off. Just what the hell everyone is looking at me for, I don't know. All I'm trying to do is get my groceries, the dog's groceries, and a couple of dishes in the process. Can't a girl do that in peace?

Oh, I know what it is. It's because of how I look. Well, so what. I was made to become this by incident. He would beat me, and it all started when I was twenty-one. I thought I was grown, too! I mean, I really thought I was hot stuff! My hair I wore really long, down to the small of my back. That's the way my man liked it. My life was so much about pleasing him that I would purposely wake up about thirty minutes ahead of him each morning so I could brush my teeth, wash up and put on make-up just so he wouldn't have to see my lesser made self. He appreciated it, too, from my vantage point.

"Well?" I swear this lady has some serious issues going on. She's just standing up here looking at me in my face like she can't read her own register. "How much is it?" My attitude is this close from taking all my items for free and rolling up out of here.

"Fifty dollars, ma'am. Just fifty dollars."

"Well, are you going to hold your hand out, or are you afraid to touch me?"

"No…," the cashier stammers, "No, ma'am. I just was in a daze for a minute is all. Please, forgive me." The cashier holds out her well manicured fingers to slowly remove the fifty dollar bill from my finger tips. I notice how she takes the very corner of the bill to make sure her fingers don't touch mine.

"Well?" I ask again, staring at the items that I just bought on the counter waiting to be bagged. Then, I look back up at everyone inside the store, and they're all looking back at me...well, at my blackened eye. Then, they scatter, pretending that their eyes weren't on me just a split second ago. Lying asses. I glare back at the cashier who is still trying to place that same fifty dollar bill in the register. "Who the hell is gonna bag…?"

"Ma'am, ma'am…here I am." The same man who blocked this register off with the buggy as soon as I got in the line earlier, is back to bag my groceries.

"Since when do managers bag groceries when the baggers are standing over there?"

"They're on break, ma'am," he says quickly as he shoves the items into about five plastic bags, not paying any attention to the order in which he places them.

"You're about to flatten my damn bread."

"So sorry, ma'am, like I said, the baggers are…"

"Move!" I grab his hand, and he snatches it away quickly. Next thing I see is him running to the bathroom. As I stare back stunned at the way people are treating me like I have some sort of airborne, deadly disease, I replace my frown with a huge smile. The bags are already separated, so I hold my other hand up to the cashier demanding she not lift another finger to help me with my groceries any further. I begin to bag the items myself.

As I'm bagging, customers pass by me, shielding their children and rushing, even dropping their own bags in the process. I simply continue to smile because they all look like train wrecks in comparison to my one black eye. My husband gave it to me yesterday, and I didn't even go to the hospital. Instead, I went to a hotel to cry it out again. Sometimes, he would get frustrated, and I would allow him to take his frustrations out on me. Stupid, I know, but I didn't know what else to do. He was the love of my life, but anyway, as far as today, I forgot my sunglasses in the car so screw it. Let the onlookers look.

When I finish filling my five bags, I place them back into my buggy, run my fingers through the top of the new hair cut I gave myself this morning, grab my shopping cart, and leave. It's like I'm a celebrity without the overflowing bank account. That's alright though because with this rate of attention, I'm bound to make the big screen one day.

My cart knocks against the floor as I push it pass the rest of the buggies that are lined up against the wall. When the sliding doors come open, as I turn to the right, my periphery catches the people that I left behind inside the store yapping on their cell phones like they've seen a ghost. I pay them no attention, continuing to walk to the silver car parked in the handicapped space. Although I'm not handicapped, I figure that I shop here enough and have earned the front spot every once in a while.

Although the only business that I'm minding is mine, cars are stopping as if I'm the latest craze in town. Even when I get across the street, my presence is causing a damn back up.

"Let me get myself back home." I adjust the rearview mirror, check my hair again and back up. That's when my cell phone begins to ring again, and it's the same number – my brother. He's been calling and calling ever since early this morning like when he talked to me the night before I didn't already tell him that I'm too busy to continue our conversation. Therefore, instead of answering it, I turn on the music full blast and jam all the way down the street.

As I ride, on the dash is a framed photo of me and my man that I snatched up from the house before I left to remind me of us. There was a time when I used to love him so much. A tear rolls down my cheek, and I almost run the red light. My foot hits the brake hard, and our framed photo almost goes crashing down until I grab it. When I do, the edge of the frame stabs me.

"Shit!" A wound on my hand opens up again from the metal digging deeply into it, and blood starts to drip into the cup holders that sit right in front of my gear shift. In order to stop my blood from dripping, I place my finger inside my mouth and suck, and that's when the light turns green again.

"That's better." My house is about one and a half blocks away, and it's only after I go through the green light that I see cars following me. The tailing is confirmed when I pull into my neighborhood, so I stop the car and lean my head out of the window. "You want something?" As I peer back into the first car, the lady ducks her head, but I can tell she has a cell phone in her hand. "Crazy ass. I tell you what though," I complain, sitting back down comfortably and continuing to drive toward my house that's at the end of the street. "No one better come on my property, and I mean no one."

When I get close enough, I push the garage remote and pull inside. My cell phone goes off again, so I pick up.

"Hello?"

"Lisa, I've been trying to call you all morning!"

"My phone has been on, and it's just turning noon. I got no calls from you," I respond, taking my things from the car. Finally being shielded from the outside world momentarily inside the garage of my home makes me feel more at ease.

"Lisa, stop playing. I'm talking about earlier this morning, like between seven thirty and nine o'clock. I was ringing the phone off the hook, so why didn't you answer?"

"That early, my phone was on silent because I didn't want to be bothered, plus my brother was lighting up my phone, too," I respond, opening the door of the house that leads to the kitchen. "Why were you calling me so much?"

"I needed to let you know that my flight won't come in until later on today, so will that conflict with anything that you have to do later because I need you to pick me up…"

"No, I can still pick you up," I answer while noticing that my countertop is a mess, but whatever. "I just have some cleaning up to do is all, but give me a call when your flight is in so I can come on out. Did you enjoy yourself?"

"Everything went perfect! Can't wait to tell you about it face to face. Gotta go, so love ya! Bye!"

"Bye, Candyce. See you soon." I hang up the phone and then end up hearing a bunch of noise outside my door. When I look outside the living room window, the street is becoming covered with people pointing, but before I can do anything else, the baby starts to whimper.

Chapter 2

"Listen, Candyce, stay off of the phone. We're getting ready to go back to the hotel. Don't go back over there and call another soul, got it?" Jack looks around out of paranoia and then takes another sip of his soda which happens to be his fifth one today.

"Alright already! Stop being so uptight. We've done this before, and no one has ever found out okay. This is just a small snag, but the next flight should be just as legit as the last one. We just board the plane as usual, and we'll be back in the United States by sundown. Be cool." Candyce leans back in her chair and crosses her legs high. Then, she places her wide brim straw hat back on to keep her facial appearance as low profile as she can. Nothing is ever one hundred percent full proof, and after the first flight is delayed, although she isn't showing it, it has put her a little bit on edge.

"No, thank you," Jack fans the waitress away before she brings refills.

"I said chill," Candyce responds, a bit irritated with the way Jack is behaving. "We'll move right through customs. It won't be a big deal. This is our only shot to get back and make the transaction, so stay cool. Stop pumping yourself up with so many sodas."

"I never had this much on me that's all. This is too much, C."

Candyce leans up toward the table as she strokes her long blond wig and purposely knocks the soda over onto his shirt and pants. "And now you have even more on you."

"What the hell!" he yells, tilting so far back in the chair that he nearly tips over onto the sidewalk.

"We're wearing butt pads, dope. If they pat us down, they'll feel nothing but ass." She then rolls her eyes at him and then stands to leave. "Let's go." As she walks away, she continues, "And I'll have on an extra set of tits."

When they get back to the hotel with Jack still wiping the drink from his pants and shirt, they take the stairs back up to their room in order to review how to go undetected at the airport. Even when they get back to the United States, Candyce has to continue her deception beyond the one person who is picking her up from the airport – Lisa. Lisa has no clue about the drug trafficking, and Candyce wants it to stay that way. She wants her friendship with Lisa to remain intact and innocent, not marred with crime. Jack, who happens to be the boyfriend that goes bananas when under pressure, isn't too keen on the idea of having Lisa pick them up. However, he goes along with the plan instead of taking a cab. Candyce has convinced him that getting Lisa to pick them up in her car saves time so that they can drop her back off at the house and then continue to drop the drugs where they should be, having a super alibi that is absolutely clueless.

"So look," Candyce continues as she sits on the bed to remove her sandals and put her hair up in a ponytail. "The plan is to appear tired and drained, yet happy, from partying it up over here on this island. It's freaking spring break, so everyone is down here, therefore, there's a lot of through traffic. We will be in and out, just like last year."

"Yeah, but what if this fake butt falls off of me. I don't even know how to move with something like this on."

"You just sit on it, dummy. Walk and sit. We're not even running. Walk, sit, walk, sit. Simple. If they touch you, pat you down even, it will feel just like a damn butt. Got it? We only got one kilo on us max, okay, Jack? Between our private parts, what could go wrong?"

Jack looks at her with disgust. "When I got here, I really believed you when you said it was going to be a vacation and not what we did last year, Candyce." He drags his hair to the other side of his head, covering the shaved portion of his scalp.

"And oh yeah. Wear your hair just like that at the airport. Make your hair work for you. Don't look like you have the potential of getting high because you know how people see others with alternative hair dos."

"Exactly! And if you would have told me about this little plan you had to make some money, I would have never shaved my damn head! I know it attracts attention, C, so don't worry. This scalp won't even show because I'm not trying to go to dang jail down here in Jamaica."

"Good, because I'm not either." She reaches across to the bag and pulls out his male butt pads. "Here. Pull them up so I can feel. I made sure that I secured some of the stuff in both cheeks so it won't look lop sided. You don't have too much, but you have just enough. Let me see. The butt pads are removable, so I think this will be a winner because I sized them up just like the pads and even the original pads fit right back in."

Jack drops his pants as Candyce keeps track of time on her watch. He then pulls up the briefs, and when he sees the way it looks in the mirror, he smiles. "This isn't half bad, C. Good job. Wanna smack it?"

"Uhhh, no. I want you to sit on it for a while and then get back up, just to make sure we don't have a buster on us. That would suck, wouldn't it?" she laughs.

"Not funny at all, comedian with absolutely no talent nor audience." Jack then pulls up his real underwear over it and then his pants. From the there he walks around and sits. "Not bad though."

"Not bad at all. Check out my breasts." She shakes. "Well padded." She stands up with a smirk as she removes her hot, blond wig. "Now, it's time for me to pack on more of my ass."

Chapter 3

"I know. I got your food, Smack. Your mom will be back today, and you can hang out around her leg until you go to sleep. Here." I put the puppy treats down next to Candyce's puppy who has been crying for food this morning because she wouldn't eat the kind that I'd bought for her the night before, thus, she's starving. I figure to just forget the dog food and get some treats. All dogs love a treat…including the other dog lying on the floor next to Smack.

"Let's go over here, Smack. You're stepping in all this blood." I move the treats over to the hallway, and then I grab the bleach, vinegar and baking soda from underneath the bathroom cabinet. While Smack is sopping up the treats, I stare back at the mess. There's so much blood on the walls and the hardwoods that I don't know where to start first, but I start.

Grabbing each and every towel that I have inside the closet, I step over Smack while she smacks, pour the bleach and water onto the kitchen floor, and start to mop. The blood spreads everywhere, including right back where it came from – inside Robert.

"I'm too tired for this shit." I grab a seat in my living room and look at my watch. "Looks like they're out there about to have a block party in the broad daylight, but right out in front of my house, though? It would have been nice if they invited us, huh, Robert?" I ask my dead husband. "Oh but wait…you wouldn't have taken me, would you have?" I turn around and ask his lifeless body. "No," I answer for him as I turn my attention back to the window. "You would've taken that damn broad you have

25

back there in our bed, but her ass can't even talk now, much less breathe, just like your ass."

There's a silver tray that once belonged to my great grandmother. It's a family heirloom, and until this day, I still use it for the same thing my grandmother and mother used it for – candy. This week, I have peppermint inside the tray, so as I lean over the tray to pick through the various flavors of candy, I see the reflection of my face inside the mirror at the bottom of the tray. Then, I'm startled by the sound of police sirens coming closer and closer. Smack is in the background chewing like a mad dog, and everything around me becomes amplified, even the people on the street. As they are pointing at my house, the crowd no longer looks like a block party. They are staring directly into the front of my window as I sit gazing back at them. I look down into the silver tray once again. Suddenly, I see the blood. It's covering me.

Quickly, I stand up and look back out into the crowd of people. That's when I notice the police cars coming at the beginning of the street. My heart skips a beat.

"Shit!" I look back around at Robert, laid out in a puddle of blood, and seconds later, I run toward the curtains and yank them shut. "I can't get out the front door!" Turning in circles, I see my car keys and purse on the edge of the kitchen counter, so I run to snatch them up along with Smack who is still smacking up the dog food. Before I run out the back door, I remember the woman I killed. That's when I rush back to my room to make sure that what I'm thinking is real, and it is. There's the woman that was laying inside my bed with my husband, and I killed her, just like I killed him, except she was easier to defeat. Her head is still dangling off of the bed. "Shit!"

With Smack in my arms, I leave out the back sliding door where my car is parked. I toss Smack over into the backseat, then I jump in the front, and without a plan, I drive right through my neighbor's backyard onto another street, leaving my house behind. I'm almost a wanted woman, so the first thing I do is call my aunt.

"Ma!" I call my aunt my mom ever since my mom passed away. They're identical twins, so whenever I see my aunt, I see my mom. It helps.

"Hey, baby girl. You sound winded."

"It's because I am, ma. I am. What are you doing right now?"

"Unloading some groceries. Why? Are you coming over?"

"Yes, I'm coming over, but I need to borrow Uncle Joe's car for a little bit, if it's not too much trouble."

"Well, what's wrong with your car, Lisa? You need some..."

"No, I don't." I knock Smack back down into the back seat because she continues to lick me on my elbow while I'm trying to drive. That's when I notice the blood all on my arm. "Shit!"

"Excuse me?"

"Not you, ma. I'll call you back." I hang up my cell phone and pull behind a plaza so that Smack can clean me up...literally. She's already started the job so why not finish. "Smack, Smack, come here, girl. Right here, right here, baby girl, good girl," I encourage her until I see some bottled waters sitting outside the back of the building. "Please, let there be some water in those bottles."

Jumping out of the car, Smack nearly gets smacked by the car door as I close it behind myself in a mad dash for the bottled water before anyone sees me. I can hear the traffic far too well on the other side of the building, but I'm shielded from mostly any other passers-by due to a thick wad of bushes.

"Come on, come on," I stress while shaking bottle after bottle until I find one that's half full. Immediately, I open it up and pour it on my face and arms. After it empties, I go on another hard search to find more water until I see it – a water hose. In a burst of energy, I turn it on and start to soak myself from top to bottom, watching the redness run down my skin until all that's left is my natural brown skin color.

When I'm all done, I drop the hose, turn the water completely off, and jump back into driver mode. "Sorry, Smack. It was either clean or be cleaned by the cops. I just murdered two people, and one of them was your Uncle Robert." I press hard on the gas. "The other one was his girlfriend, and she asked for it because she was in my bed as a fucking intruder. She's lucky I couldn't kill her ass twice."

Tears disappear into my face as it blends with the evaporating moisture from my drenched face. I'm not even crying because I murdered my husband or his mistress. I'm crying because I'm going to get caught because I actually went to the damn grocery store covered in blood.

As I drive down back roads, checking for signs of anyone chasing me while thanking God that I have tinted windows although I know He probably doesn't hear me right now, I glance continuously at my clothing. My tan shirt looks like I dropped loads of tomato sauce onto it, and my jeans look like a paint job gone wrong. My sneakers feel like I'm pushing on a load of baby wipes soaked in diarrhea because of all the water that gushes from them when I make any type of movement.

I rub my right hand back and forth on the passenger's seat to dry it off and then start to dial Ma once again. I'm only two minutes away from her house, and this is probably the fifth to last place the cops will look for me. I've never lived with her at all, but like I said earlier, I call her Ma since mine is gone now.

Chapter 4

"Shut the door!" Candyce yells at Jack as he slowly enters the taxi. Her face is beet red on her pale skin as she looks at her boyfriend with a severe case of the slaps. Then, she whispers as she leans over his way like she's giving him a kiss so the driver won't get suspicious. "Sorry for yelling, baby, it's just that..." she continues, moving closer to his ear. "You better not mess this shit up."

Jack pays her no attention but just stares straight ahead, shoving his body closer to the window.

"Just to the airport?" asks the taxi driver.

"Yes, sir. To the airport it is." She grabs Jack's hand. "I really am sorry, baby. Please forgive me. I didn't mean to do what I did," she lies just to throw the cab driver off in case he's a rat.

"You just don't listen! You always have to take things so lightly when this is some heavy stuff, Can..."

"I only had sex with one guy!" She glares at Jack for forcing her to lie once again atop concealing her real name that he was just about to blurt out. "I won't do it again, I swear." She bats her eyes away from the taxi driver whom she notices is looking at them much more than before, therefore, she decides to quiet down. Jack, on the other hand, struggles to remain at peace, with a load of dope strapped to his butt cheeks, on his way to the airport.

As soon as they arrive, they both count to five after the cab driver gets out to help them unload their things.

"Go," Candyce responds as she spots her major connect down the sidewalk. Jack spots him as well, and it places him in a rage once again because of the way the guy looks at Candyce. Although Candyce was assumed to be lying about sleeping with only one person while in Jamaica, Jack thinks that she may be telling the truth. It's all because of sir stare-a-lot down the sidewalk.

"I'm sick of his shit."

"Well, stop stepping in it, and let's go," Candyce whispers. "Thank you so much, and you have a great day. We had so much fun over here!" Candyce explains gleefully to the cab driver as he waves and gets back into his car. Then, she orders Jack to grab his bag off the street and follow her. Instead, he grabs his bag and starts to walk toward the major drug connect down the sidewalk. "What in the world?"

"Yeah, bro. I'm coming for you," Jack steams, storming down the walkway towards a man who could kill him in one blink of his eyes. "Always taking your eyes up and down my lady, but before I leave here today, I'm gonna knock those eyes down your throat. That's a promise."

Lugging her suitcase behind her, Candyce speeds up to catch her man before he gets them busted. This is the only time they can make the drop, so it's now or never. She watches as the drug connect stands tall and flicks the cigarette from his hand to only place that same hand on his pocket. This prompts Candyce to drop her luggage and shove Jack into a standstill.

"What," she begins, moving her hair from her face, "is your problem? You're going to attract too much attention. Now act like you have some sense before he shoots you where you stand, and then I end up in jail over here," she says grinding her teeth. Then, she looks back

31

over to the connect, smiles, takes Jack's hand, and then turns him back around. They both walk back toward the main entrance of Sangster International airport. People are everywhere, but Candyce keeps it quite cool considering she's sweating due to Jack's little dumb stunt. As they pass through the doors, Candyce warns, "Keep your shit together. Act a fool when we get into the car with Lisa all you want, but until then, shut the hell up. Just what the hell was that stunt you pulled back there?"

"You slept with someone, huh?'"

"What?" Candyce continues walking hand in hand with him with a huge smile on her face as a big front to onlookers. Jack looks pleasant as well now, the further he gets into the airport.

"What you said in the cab. You slept with him, didn't you…when you went in the other room the other night to get the goods?" He cuts his eyes at her and then taps her butt.

"Are you crazy?" She laughs pleasantly but inside her heart, she wants to take a chair and go upside his head. "That was a diversion you idiot. I couldn't do that if you were in the other room…even if I wanted to. Sure, he's attracted to me, but that's a good thing. You're not walking around with an ugly ass, so be happy."

As they stand in line, Jack fumes and forgets that he has his hair laid to the side to hide his shaved scalp when he runs his hand through it. Immediately, he catches the dire look Candyce gives him and knows what she's so anxious about, but it's too late. They're at the counter. The clerk speaks and continues about her work, getting their ticket information for the flight straight, while Candyce and Jack pretend to be interested in getting more souvenirs.

Jack notices the attendant glance at his appearance and then at Candyce's, but she says nothing.

"Do any of your bags need to be checked?" the clerk asks with a huge commercial smile.

"Yes, please, all three."

"What are the contents of the bag, please?"

"Clothing, shoes and curling irons."

"Thank you," she says as she takes the bag. "And you, sir?"

"Clothing is all."

"Thank you." She then takes his luggage and hands them both their boarding passes and identification. "Have a great trip back to the United States."

"Thank you so much. We enjoyed our stay." They both walk away, hand in hand, privately packed with a kilo of cocaine, ready to board the plane. "We'll be home in two and a half hours tops. Florida here we come."

They board the flight with no hang-ups from customs.

Chapter 5

"Just what the heck happened to you, Lisa, and do you have another migraine?" Ma asks as I rush both myself and Smack inside the house. "Oh no you don't, sweetheart! Put that dog on the deck out back. You know better than that. No pets…"

"In this house." I complete the sentence for her. "And yeah, I have another migraine." I adjust the cataract sunglasses on my face that I lied to get for free from the doctor. I told him that I kept getting migraines every time I look at or near the sun, so he prescribed me meds which I never take and gave me a pair of old people sunglasses that are actually used for concealing the truth of my abusive relationship from my relatives, friends and strangers. They literally cover my eyebrows all the way down to my cheekbones along with the sides of my eyes like a gladiator with no style whatsoever. "Ma, can I borrow a shirt or something?"

"And what did you do to your hair? You cut it all off?" Ma scopes me over, and even I don't know what to say about it except…

"Gum and syrup. I was watching some children earlier and when I went to sleep, they got me. Look…at me," I stammer but the lie goes together perfectly. "I even had tomato sauce all over my clothes so I hosed off, cussed out the kids and left them with their mom when she got home to beat their little asses…"

"Lisa!"

"Sorry, ma. But now I'm late because I have to pick up Candyce from the airport."

"Right now?"

"Yes, Ma, and I'm sorry but you were the closest to me. My car is all wet inside, so can I use Uncle Joe's for a while? I'll bring it right back." The clock is hanging high on the wall, and all I can ponder is what the hell are the cops doing in my house right now? They've had enough time to bust inside, and by now, they're looking for me in the ten minutes that it has taken me to get away. "I'll park my car in the garage."

Ma sighs, but eventually – after about five minutes of sipping her tea and digging through her purse – gives me the keys. I'm about to explode through the whole ordeal of her searching and sipping and listening to Smack bark through the screen door as panic continues to eat away at my core. She hands me the car keys.

"Please, don't mess up your uncle's car. You know that's the good car."

"I know. I'll keep it safe, and Ma...I love you. Can I get the clothes now? I really gotta go."

"Oh yeah. Be right back." She then pauses, "Come on back here with me, so you can get what you want. You better be glad we can wear the same clothes. We were always the same size."

Thus, I go back to the back bedroom where her spacious closet undermines what I think is masterful at my house to which I can never return. While I'm in the room with her as she sifts through her jeans, I tune my ears in to the news. There's nothing sounding off about my killings, so before it reaches the news, I rush my aunt by grabbing the first two pair of jeans I see and two shirts from the closet that already look ironed and ready to go.

35

"This will work right here, Ma. Thanks. I have to run. I'll have the car back in no time, and I love you…very much," I tell her, changing right in front of her face.

"I know you do, sweetheart, and love you, too. Those parents need to beat those bad ass kids though for messing you up like they did."

"Don't they?" I lightly laugh because Ma doesn't know the other half of me, Robert, is sitting in hell with his side chick, leaving me a widow. While in my fake laughter mode, I finish changing my clothes, kiss Ma on the cheek, run to snatch Smack from the deck, toss her in my uncle's car, back it out and place my soon to be wanted vehicle inside the garage, making certain I pull the garage door all the way back down. Ma and Uncle Joe have grown paranoid of carbon monoxide, so they never pull it all the way down since the neighbor sat in his car and killed himself reading the paper. He had his work clothes on and all, but forgot to open the garage. He just sat there and died.

"Leather, just what I need," I say to myself as I floor it backwards, and by the time I get to the street from the driveway, I notice I forgot to borrow some shoes. "Shit!" Nevermind. I kick them off. "What would make me put back on the same shoes…and my hair? Dang it!" I can't believe I did that. Tears stream down my face again as the gravity of the situation that I'm trying to avoid comes creeping up anyway. "I can't believe…I can't believe I did that," I repeat as I recall all the details of the events I temporarily forgot only hours ago.

**

"Come on in here, girl."

"Stop playing, Robert," she flirts as he takes her by the waist and pulls her inside the house. There is a candlelight on the dining room table with the fresh scent of flowers as well as a full dinner waiting. After closing the door behind her, he escorts her over to the table that is completely set, pulls her chair out and is sure she is comfortable when she takes her seat in front of her T-bone steak, steamed vegetables, baked potato and rice with a glass of expensive wine.

"I prepared this all for you, sweetheart." He kneels down at her feet and stares into her eyes. "You're special to me, and I know that I haven't taken it where I need to take it. I just want you know that I will." He places his hand on hers and rubs her ring finger. "One day, it's going to be me and you."

"Only me and you?" she smiles.

"Come here." He leans in to his girlfriend's face and gives her a warm, loving kiss on the lips. She smiles and takes it all in as she begins to cry from becoming so overwhelmed with desire for the one and only man she loves.

Robert then pulls back and welcomes her to eat as he sits next to her. They both enjoy the food, romance, and joy that comes with the night. By the time they finish eating, the clock strikes eleven, and they migrate their naked bodies to his bedroom.

They can't keep their hands off one another as they get tangled up in the clothing that drops to the floor as they stumble to the bed. Behaving like two wild animals, they rush each other into the entertainment of their lives. There is a stereo adjacent to the king sized bed that is layered in red satin sheets, and when they fall onto the slippery place of rest, relaxation and sex, he reaches over and presses play, already having the songs set for the night. One of their favorites start the playlist – Let's Get It On by Marvin Gaye – and they get it on up through the early hour of two o'clock in the morning. This is when the front door unlocks.

The music has already stopped playing when a woman with a black eye walks inside the house. She sits her purse down at the door and simply stands there eyeballing the dinner she made for her man at seven o'clock in the evening. The candlelight is completely melted down, and the T-Bone steaks that she made for the both of them are completely demolished. As she approaches to get a closer look, she notices a woman's clutch tilted at the leg of the dining room chair. Along with that, as she turns toward the noise coming from the bedroom, she spots different clothing items scattered about from where she stands to the beginning of the hallway.

As she glances back at the window, she notices the blinds are wide open. The street is quiet, and although she just came into the house, she isn't aware of the time. Therefore, she looks at the clock which reads five minutes after two o'clock in the morning. A tear falls from her black eye, and she walks over slowly to close the living room blinds.

Suddenly, she hears her friend's puppy, Smack, hungry and needing some water, so she walks over and dumps the food into the bowl and fills the water bowl beside it. Assuming that the puppy is satisfied, she washes her hands and opens the utensil drawer to pull out a knife, the biggest one she has. From there, she opens the single car garage door to see if another car is inside besides the silver one. There isn't. Robert's car is unusually parked on the street in front of the house while she has already parked her car in the back, behind the house.

She hears more noise coming from the back room, therefore, she continues to move pass Smack who is messing over the dog food in her hunger, and enters the hallway where she hears the sound of a woman's giggle from inside her bedroom. She wipes the tears from her injured face as she steps in front of the cracked bedroom door. There they are.

Her husband Robert is holding a woman in his arms, the way he would hold her when he wasn't beating and chasing her out of the house. As she stands there and watches, her heart begins to crumble, but for some reason, it won't stop beating. Therefore, she continues into the room quietly as she watches them caress and kiss one another inside the satin sheets that she purchased only four months ago. It was for Valentine's Day.

She walks up to them both, and they are so consumed with one another in the darkness that they don't even see her although she stands directly inside the light that enters the window from a huge night light that is located at the back of the neighbor's house. When she walks closer to the bed, so close that her knees touch the mattress, she inspects how her husband Robert is cradling his girlfriend. The woman is settled comfortably in his groin area as his arms are wrapped around her. Both their eyes are completely shut, but they are still awake because they are whispering to one another. Robert's back is turned toward his wife as she listens to him tell the woman lying in the bed with him the worst thing that she could possibly hear – *I love you.*

That's enough. She grips the knife tightly, her tears completely dried up, reaches over the both of them and slits the woman's throat from one end to the other as she lies there unprotected by her husband. Blood streams everywhere, and Robert lets go of his girlfriend only to stare back into the desperately insane and enraged eyes of his wife that he beat up hours ago. Within seconds as the woman's naked body flips over to try and save her own life, Robert glances at her struggle but then panics as his own wife stands over him without saying a word. The knife says it all. He then jumps his naked body off of the bed, but doesn't make it completely off before his young, thirty year old wife digs the knife into his side, retrieves it and then stabs him again in his back.

Robert doesn't fall. He only stumbles as he reaches for a wall to hold himself up, but his wife trips him up with her foot, causing him to bust his face against the edge of the doorway. She smirks, but doesn't utter a sound, thinking about all the food she cooked for him hours ago, the way she cleans up constantly so that he can come home to a real home, the way she consistently tried to get pregnant, run his bath water, iron his clothes and even do without so that he can do with. Finally, as she watches him mop the hallway's hardwoods with his own flesh and blood in an attempt to escape, she figures that the only way she can get her life back is to take his away. By the time Robert makes it beyond the living room screaming for help, she walks up to him as the puppy Smack begins to lick his face in the kitchen. She then stabs him once more in the back of the neck.

Smack continues to lick him until Lisa, Robert's wife, picks the puppy up to place her in a back room. Then, Lisa takes a seat at the dining room table to feast on the leftovers from her well cooked meal.

Chapter 6

"These seats suck."

"You're always complaining. Just think about something else and stop talking. We're almost back in Florida, so chill alright?"

"I'm going to the bathroom."

"Bye," Candyce retorts, as Jack unbuckles himself to head to the back of the airplane. "I'm glad he's gone. A freaking nuisance," she whispers to herself as the man in the seat in front of her peers backwards just to be nosey. Before shutting her eyes to relax, she catches him looking and pretends to cross her legs but kicks his chair instead. He then turns back around to mind his own business as she calls him out his name. "Beast."

As Jack makes it to the airline's bathroom, he has to wait for someone else to get out. When it finally becomes empty, he nods to the person exiting, and then goes directly inside. Instead of urinating or defecating, he shuts the lid, washes his hands, and then sits down on top of it and all the drugs he's smuggling right up against his buttocks.

"What's the purpose of giving her this when I just know I'm gonna be in the damn penitentiary behind her ass?" He pulls the thirty thousand dollar diamond from his pocket and looks at it sparkling on the band. Although she takes him through changes, he adores Candyce very much, so much that he believes marrying her is the perfect thing for him to do right now. The plan was to go to Jamaica to vacation, and on the vacation, Jack planned on proposing until he got pulled into her scheme of drug trafficking to get a jump on what she considers a flaccid bank account back in the United States. It destroyed his plans. Being more of a romantic than Candyce, the whole vibe was ruined for him, so he pushed his proposal to the backburner. "All the trouble I went through…"

As he sits back quite heartbroken at the fact that going through with the drug deal could ruin their relationship and his life forever, he thinks back to the one and only other thing that could still get him arrested and sent away to prison. It all happened in Orlando…

**

Crossing the street in the only dapper suit in his closet, he spots the only jewelry store on the block. Although he doesn't have any money, good credit or much less a job, he decides to live a little like a wealthy man. No one will know the difference, and in order to become the part, he was always told by his mom to act the part. Acting will carry anyone a long way, she would say, and after that, the jig is up. Well, Jack's acting skills were up to par this particular day, and to him, it felt good.

As soon as he steps onto the curb and places his body directly in front of the jewelry store doors, he checks his hair in the reflection. It's long but neat, and after he sees that he is as clean as a whistle, he goes inside. The place is a rich people kind of quiet, where the customers are talking in high pitched, soprano voices and smiling at one another with the fake laughs that speak nothing but money. Jack walks by each of them, remaining silent and nodding to those he sees, being sure to look them in the eyes with that all-together-and-making-it-happen, commanding-yet-willing-to-let-you-lead look. He notices that all the jewelry is kept in immaculate condition, but even if it isn't well kept, he can't tell. That's what the act is for.

"Are you in search of anything special this afternoon, sir? We have remarkable new arrivals here and even more remarkable items in the back, if you would tell me how I may be of service to you?"

After his tongue unlocks from his jaw, Jack responds with a flashy smile and calm demeanor, "I'm in love. What type of ring would you like?"

"Are you asking me?" the jeweler asks, figuring he's full of jokes as she continues to move to the more expensive engagement rings three steps to her right. Then, she unlocks the thick glass cabinet.

Jack spins around and knocks on the glass three times, looks at his fake Rolex that he got off the corner the week prior, and then glances back at her. He notices how she glances at the watch for a split second before placing her attention back on the jewels in front of her.

"So you're a Rolex man I see?"

"Is that a question or a statement?"

"Both."

"For the most part." He then yanks on the bottom of his suit's sleeve to emphasize the fact that he has one on, no matter how fake. "So which would you prefer?" he asks, glossing over the rings.

"Of all these," she answers, picking up a two carat, thirty thousand dollar diamond solitaire, "this diamond is of magnificent quality, and I personally adore it." She sits it down atop the glass counter directly in front of her body, and glances in another direction toward other rings. "Now we have more two carat rings over there, however, the quality of those diamonds don't stand to compare to one that's meant for the love of your life."

Jack stands there quietly thinking about the thirty thousand dollars that he doesn't have. In his mind, he thinks about all the things that thirty thousand dollars can buy, and he really doesn't see what's so special about the ring that would make it cost more than most cars. Then he figures it out – love.

"Well, quality is everything when it comes to love. I'll take it, and I'll take it right now." Before the jeweler even answers, he turns around one more time and faces the door. Then, he retrieves his wallet, holds it up to his chest, hits it twice, then turns back around.

"A man who knows what he wants for his lady. How will you be paying for this, Mr…"

"Walton. James Walt…"

"Everybody against the back walls, now!" Three men with masks and guns enter the store shouting. "Customers down on the floor, let's go!"

As the jeweler stands there horror stricken at what she recognizes as a heist, she doesn't notice the man she knows as Mr. Walton standing there looking at her calmly as he places his hand atop the ring and drops to the floor, the thirty thousand dollar solitaire inside his left palm. He pretends to be afraid, but not while remaining stagnant on the floor with the others. Instead, he quickly wiggles his way to the front door beyond the gunmen's feet with his head tilted away from the other camera, stands and runs out the door. He never looks back, and he never meets his friends again with whom he planned the heist. That was the plan. Do it, split, and never speak again for five years. Let the case grow cold.

**

"And all the friends I lost…and I gotta stay lost."
He reaches under his butt. "I gotta get this shit off my ass."
He thinks about it once more, stands up off of the toilet,
puts the diamond engagement ring back inside his pants
pocket, securing it with a safety pin, and then slides his
pants down. "I gotta stay out of prison. If they match my
face up with the heist after catching me with these drugs,
I'm in prison for longer than I can count," he whispers to
himself. "Besides that, there's no way we can make it
through customs again in the United States. No way."

Jack pulls down the padded butt cheeks that
Candyce padded up with the cocaine, takes them
completely off, and picks them up off the floor. All he can
think about are the dogs that will smell the scent a mile
away, and he stuffs the whole entire thing in the trash can.
It was luck being able to board in Jamaica without getting
caught. When he pulls back up his regular underwear and
pants, he turns to stare at the dope he just put down. He
changes his mind.

"No," he sighs frustrated, so he pulls his pants back
down and yanks the tight padded fake butt cheeks back up
and redresses. "I'll dump this crap in the airport. No way
in hell I'm going to prison…no way. Not with this damn
rock," he says referring to the ring he lifted for Candyce.

Finally, he flushes the toilet, pretending that he used
it for anyone who may be waiting in the wing. When he
opens the door, no one is there, so he turns to walk back to
his seat. Before he gets there, he spots Candyce's head,
and he nearly gags because he's still bothered by the fact
that she really could have slept with another man while on
vacation. He puts his hand down inside his pants pocket

45

and squeezes the ring tightly, giving everything about his life second and third thoughts.

He makes it to his seat, sits and says, "I almost threw the stuff out."

Candyce doesn't even hear him. She's too busy staring out the window and listening to music, so he speaks directly into her ear while pulling the earplugs off of her head.

"I almost threw it out."

She snatches away from him and looks around at all the people on the flight. Then she turns and bulges her eyes back at him, sifting each word through her teeth and pinched lips. "Seriously? Seriously, Jack?"

He just stares at her, hoping that she understands the magnitude of confusion and fear groping him at his backside. Unfortunately, she doesn't and angrily rips a pen from her small purse, pulls out a restaurant receipt and writes in all caps…

I KNOW THE PERSON AT CUSTOMS IN FLORIDA, DUMMY. WE AIN'T GETTIN' CAUGHT!

Jack wildly snatches the note from her after reading it, insulted by the whole nightmare she's putting him through. He's not the most innocent person in the universe, but he still can't believe he's in love with a full out villain with a ton of secrets.

"Just when the hell were you gonna tell me?"

"I wasn't. You just happened to give me no choice, with your loud ass."

"Why wouldn't you say anything about that?" he stresses, his hands going completely haywire like he's batting a bumble bee or a fly.

"Because you're a damn control freak, and I'm trying to get you to calm down with that stuff. It's a complete turn off, and you are such a drag when you aren't living on the impulse." She puts her earphones back on her ears and begins to rest again. He snatches them off of her head and tosses them to the floor. Candyce doesn't flinch, but she feels every red blood cell inside her veins begin to clot up from holding back the pure rage of wanting to slam his head against the beast's chair that sits in front of her.

"Impulse? Impulse?" Jack grits his teeth and the veins in his left hand bulge like a superhero's as he points his finger into her face, nearly touching the tip of her narrow nose. "This ain't the shit that's supposed to be impulsive," he scowls.

"Oops, where is it?" she smiles as she pulls the bottom of his shirt up to her nostril while the flight attendant walks by staring at Jack confused on why he is allowing her to clean out her nostril with his shirt.

"Ma'am, would you like a pack of tissue? I have some…"

"Yes, please." Candyce responds totally excited as she reaches over and takes the tissue from the gracious attendant. "I thought I had a nose bleed, but I'm fine. Just a scratch. Thanks, babe, for pointing that out," she comments to Jack who smiles a bit, shrugs his shoulder and nods at the attendant with really nothing to say…but he says something anyway.

"Just a little smear," he says as he rubs his thumb onto the spot on his shirt where Candyce dug up her nostril.

"Would you like some hand sanitizer, sir?" asks the flight attendant who is obviously grossed out but trying desperately hard not to show it.

"Oh, yes, please. I have to drop her off at a party when she gets home, and it was either my clothes or hers," he lies.

"Oh, okay. Here you are." She squirts some hand sanitizer in his hand, and then comments. "That was sweet."

"It's always good to have a mister macho around!" Candyce adds. Then, she squints her eyes and says, "Thanks again."

The attendant nods and continues on her stroll.

"Fuck you, Candyce."

"Likewise."

Chapter 7

"Oh now what!" I shout out loudly, thundering through the traffic yet careful to do the speed limit while becoming frantic as my cell phone rings again. It's my brother again. I quickly calm my nerves, take a deep breath as I turn down another back road, and answer the phone, "Hey, Lug!"

"Don't hey me, Lisa. You're ignoring my calls again, and it sucks because I really needed to talk to you about something."

"What about? Sorry I didn't answer your call, but I was really busy…"

"You're never that busy, Lisa, so stop playing! I'm your brother, come on now."

The disappointment in Lug's voice penetrates through her chest bone to knock her directly in her heart. Robert never wanted me to have a close relationship with Lug ever since we got married. Things almost fell apart between me and my younger brother all because Robert felt jealous of my relationship with him every time we were on the phone together or went out. Robert would huff and puff when we would return to the house, despite the fact that we would always ask him to come along. He wouldn't even say a word to Lug, and even though Lug was always ready to defend me, he would stand down because of the embarrassment on my face. I would always look so nervous, and he never wanted to make things at home worse. Lug…he's always been so good at reading me. He knew I wasn't happy, but he refrained from nagging me about it. He's never seen one of my black eyes or busted lips because those were my busy times.

"I need to borrow your car."

I press on the brakes of my Uncle Joe's car, and they make a huge squeak as the car comes to a stop. "What?" I ask, my voice sunken in despair.

"I have to go to work, and my car is dead."

"What the heck happened to your car, Lug?"

"I don't know. It's just dead, and I don't have time to access the whole situation," he responds, huffing and puffing.

"Wait, what are you doing?" I ask as I sit in the middle of the street listening to the rapid breathing on the other end of the phone.

"I'm riding my bike, that's what. I'm on my way to your house because you're the closest one that can help me out."

I put the car in park and drop my hands from the steering wheel. A little girl skates in front of the car on her in-lines while her mom races to get her out of the street as she waves her hands to get my attention. I nod to let her know that I am very aware of her daughter in the road, and then I lift the cell phone, that now weighs a ton, back to my ear.

"Lisa!"

"I'm not at home, Lug." Tears start to fall from my eyes again, and I remove the cataract sunglasses from my face so the tears won't get trapped inside the rims of the thick things. I remove them too fast, however, because when the lady who chases her child looks up to thank me, her smile fades into pure shock at how red my eyeball is surrounded by the black of the knock-out punch Robert laid on me. I put back on my sunglasses, and the lady walks away with her child, disturbed. I can tell she wants to help. I start driving away so that she doesn't have the chance. She simply has no idea.

"Not at home? Dang. That means that I rode all this way for nothing. Man, I just started this job, Lisa!"

"You did? A new job?" I ask, wiping the tears off my cheeks as I ride slowly down the road.

"Yeah, sis. I don't know what to do."

I can tell that he's stopped his race to my house because his panting has come to a slow down. "How far are you away from my house? I might be able to come scoop you up. I…uhm…I'm driving Uncle Joe's car right now because Robert has my car at the moment."

"Really? You think you can do that for me? I can go ahead and finish the ride to your house so you can meet me there if you want me to…"

"No, no, no," I interject. "Just where are you? I can swing around there and get you." I hold in my cry as I think that this will probably be the last opportunity for me to see my brother. Adjusting my sunglasses, I wait on his response.

"I'm over here by the gym, the one that's…"

"I know which one. I'm coming now because I have to pick up someone from the airport. Just go over there at the side of the building, and I'll pull up, pop the trunk so you can load the bike and then we'll be off as soon as you hop inside." Pulling the phone away from my face, I sniffle, clear my throat and continue, "So that's a bet!"

"Wow! Thanks, sis. That's why I love you, girl. I'm on it right now. You're my lifesaver."

"Where is it that you work?" I ask as I spin the car around while knowing that driving back there will be extremely risky even though I know a back route. No one is looking for this car, so I figure it will be easier to dodge the cops. "You didn't tell me that you had another job."

"I know. It was supposed to be a secret, but later for the birthday surprise. I won't be able to throw myself a huge birthday bash if I don't have the money to pay for the dang thing because I lost my job."

His birthday is at the end of the month. He'll be twenty seven years old, and the most handsome little brother that any sister could ask for. Last year, I threw him a huge party to try and make up for the twenty-fifth birthday party that I missed due to my fake migraines. I had the perfect set up, and I even invited the girlfriend who later left him for another man only three months later. Regardless of that, he enjoyed every moment because at the time, all his favorite women were there – me, Ma, his girlfriend and even our real mother in video. I'd set the party up to mimic his sixteenth birthday party. It was the one that mom prepped for months to execute, and his twenty-sixth year old party, brought him so much joy. Me and Lug…we're all we have. I have no choice but to help him get to work on time. It's these little things in life that have helped us along in life – being there for each other.

"You still didn't tell me where you're working now."

"Oh yeah…Smiths & Brothers."

"The law firm? Get out of here, Lug! That's great!"

"Yeah, thanks sis. I wanted to surprise you, but don't tell anyone else, okay? I want to hold it until the party."

"You mean to tell me that you're riding a bike in a suit? No one ever walks inside that building without a dry cleaned, fully pressed three piece."

"No...I have the suit hanging off my back. I'm not that damn dumb."

Of course he isn't. He's never been as dumb as me. I flick the radio on. "Listen, I'll be there in about ten minutes, okay? Lemme drive so I won't wreck Uncle Joe's car. You know how he is."

"Wait...you got the good car?"

"Yeah, that's the one."

"How did you get..."

"Don't ask. See you in a minute at the side of the gym that faces the drug store."

"Bet."

We hang up our phones. This is a dream for Lug, but it's a nightmare for me. The day I kill Robert and his girlfriend, my brother announces that he works at a damn law firm. I turn on the radio to listen up for the news, expecting the report of a dangerous woman on the loose by the name of Lisa Caldwell. Thankfully, I still don't hear it which gives me more time to get out of here quickly.

As I pull up to the road that veers off two blocks down from my neighborhood, I don't see Lug anywhere on the street which means he did as I asked him and went to wait on me at the side of the gym. Pulling off onto the road that reaches the gym from the back way, I check on Smack who is still okay with her tongue wagging but surely, she needs a urine and poop stop. She does fairly well with the hold it and wait, but she's not to be pushed because she'll go overboard with it, making a huge pile of dung. That can't happen in Uncle Joe's car.

I used to frequent this gym so much until I know where all the cameras are located around the building. Therefore, I pull up to the back and let Smack out near this patch of dirt and grass up against the building where no one except someone extremely nosey will be able to see her lay waste. When she's done, I smack her tail and she hops back into the car. She's fast.

Removing my cataract slash migraine slash hide my black eye sunglasses, I check my eye out of paranoia. To this day and beyond, I won't allow my brother to know I was in love with a man who beats, cheats on me, and dines on my feasts with another woman, so I reach into my pocket for the flimsy pair of sun blockers that slides down behind the other sunglasses just in case.

"Crap! These aren't my pants!" I put the car in park and reach back to the floor board of the backseat to get my wet and bloody pants from the plastic bag I put them in when I changed at Ma's house. "There they are." I retrieve the flimsy piece of what feels like plastic and slide it in front of my eyes. Then I place the cataract slash migraine slash hide my black eye sunglasses back on my face. My hair is shot to death, but I can't fix that. "Let's go, Smack." I put the car in drive.

Pulling around the corner, I'm so nervous that my hands shake, but I continue for my brother's sake. When I see him, I can't help but start crying, so I stop the car. However, when I stop it, Lug turns around because of the brakes squeaking. "Stupid brakes," I sob, but immediately get myself together as he doesn't wait for me to ride closer to him. Instead, he picks up his bike, and I pop the trunk because he's heading my way. I can feel the warmth of two tears that have fallen into the sunglasses, so I scrape my finger across the bottom of the frames and flick the salt water as Lug passes by the passenger's side window. When I hear him close the trunk, I lean over onto the window, holding my head up by my arm, faking head pain.

"Thanks, big sis. Gimme some," he says leaning over for a kiss on the cheek. "Drive like you have good sense too or like you have my best suit in the back of the trunk with a bike that could crush it with a wrong turn." He looks in the back seat at Smack who is wagging her tail wildly at whom she sees as a complete stranger. "Who's this?"

"That's a friend of mine's puppy. Do you remember Candyce?"

"Yeah, I do. That blonde girl from the other day that was…"

I interject. "Yeah, her. I'm keeping her dog for her until she gets back from vacation." Lug should remember her well because he watched as her and her boyfriend Jack kissed each other in the mouth in the middle of the driveway at my house. He was terribly fascinated because they didn't come up for air for like five minutes. I left him out there watching, and he was the one that timed it. When they finished, Lug was also locked outside my house, courtesy of Robert. He forbade me from opening the door, so Lug, thinking it was my joke, got in the car and left while he called me from the cell phone laughing. I never told him that it wasn't me who locked him out. I just let it blow over.

I rub my head to lead the conversation another route.

"Lisa, get your head looked at for real. Having that many migraines each month isn't good. You got a new hair cut!" He notices the wack job I put on it. "You want me to drive?" he offers.

"No, I got it. Just lock up so I can get you there. I need to get to the airport." Just then, I think about money, and lots of it that I truly don't have. I need a flight out before they put one of those most wanted, all-points bulletins out on me. I can't even leave the country because I don't have a damn passport. I can get to Mexico though. Yes...Mexico.

"You got here just in time so I can get there good and early, throw on those clothes, and head in. Will you sit there in the parking lot so I don't have to lug a bag of clothes with me?"

"Sure," I respond rolling my eyes to keep from crying. There is this overwhelming ball of burning moisture in my throat due to the fact that if I'm caught, I have to go away for a long time. "Why do you have to go in to work so late? Are law offices open past five o'clock?"

"Well," he starts, making himself more comfortable in the chair, pulling on the tip of his nose and letting out a deep breath. "I was first invited to sit in with research for this massive murder case, you know the one that hit television last week about..."

As he rambles on, the only word that sticks out like a sore monster is murder. Suddenly, as I make my way from the parking lot to the back road that can get me away from my house and close to his job about two minutes quicker, I zoom in on the noise Smack is making in the backseat. She's vomiting. "Crap!" I totally miss what Lug is saying, leap from the car while at the stop sign, grab Smack from the back seat, and then let her finish her regurgitation on the ground. Once that finishes, I rush back into the car.

"Uncle Joe is gonna kill you, sis," Lug laughs at what I figure isn't a bit funny. I still play it cool instead of blowing up because it's not his fault that he doesn't know he's riding with a fugitive.

"I'll clean it up before he gets it back," I conclude over his laughter.

When we finally arrive at his new job, he kisses me on my hand like the wanna be player that he is, and then asks me one thing, "Can a brother get a ride back home? I'll call you later, okay, to let you know what time if I don't end up already having a ride."

"Sure," I lie while staring my little brother back in his handsome face. I'll just take his bike back to his apartment and head out while the cops have a cold trail on me. "I love you, and whatever you do today, make it count towards your future."

"Oh you know that, sis!" he responds with his fresh new hair cut and extremely low, taped up mustache while he wears a hint of cologne which doesn't smell bad even though it's mixed with his evaporated sweat that came from riding the bike to the gym. "Bye!"

57

"Bye baby boy."

The door slams, and I turn my head quickly as I erupt into tears. Although every news station will probably have my picture up, I have no getaway plan and will soon have no family if I get caught. My heart begins to send me into a panic attack, and my chest begins to move up and down so rapidly that I can't seem to take any air in. Pushing the air conditioning on full blast, I stop thinking about how I'm going to get to Mexico from Florida. The safest place, the only place I can go right now, is to Lug's place until I can sort things out. Uncle Joe keeps a full tank of gas, so I wipe my eyes and pull out into the intersection, thankful that I don't have to stop anywhere to fill up. My face could be anywhere.

When I get to Lug's apartment, I hurry and lift his bike to the front door, careful to keep my head down. Only a few people have seen me at his place, namely his next door neighbors, and I'm glad they're nowhere to be seen. As I unlock the door with his spare key that he let me have for just in case moments like this one, Smack starts barking from the car. Therefore, I put the bike at the entrance on its kickstand so I can run and snatch Smack out of the car before she attracts unwanted attention. Luckily, when I get there, she quiets down as soon as she sees my face, and she wags her tail wildly even after I shut the apartment door behind us. That's when I drop her to the floor at the sight of Lug's once empty apartment.

"What the hell?"

Lug's apartment is decked out with brand new leather furniture, oil paintings, and even rugs to cover the hardwoods. His place used to only have one raggedy loveseat with a big ass hole in the back of it that he hid from everyone when he pushed it against the wall, a couple of metal chairs, and a card table that he used to eat and do his homework. As I watch Smack slide on the surprisingly polished hardwood floor, my eyes immediately meet the television that sits atop a brand new, wide, wooden shelf.

"How the hell can he afford this when he just got that job?" I whisper while I walk over to the blinds and close them all the way shut. Lug has always had a bad habit of leaving the blinds halfway closed ever since we were kids, but being his older sister, I always went behind him to straighten them out. I suppose that's one reason why he never learned better.

Instead of continuing to wonder where Lug got the money to buy all this new merchandise in just thirty damn days, which was the last time I recall really coming inside the apartment, I flick on the big ass television and turn nervously to one of the news channels. "Come on, come on," I strain while taking off my cataract sunglasses. The television finally comes on, and the volume is up full blast. I fumble the remote control, and it falls to the floor. By the time I pick it back up, my heart is going a mile a minute, so I hit mute before turning the volume down and go grab a glass of water from the kitchen. That's when I see a plastic bag full of credit cards and identification cards in the drawer jutting out beside the dishwasher. Then, my heart collapses as I glance back at the television, and my phone rings.

Chapter 8

"We're finally here, so look for the lady with the light red tint in her hair, Jack."

"What? Why should I look for her? I thought you said you knew her," he forcefully whispers as they exit the aircraft to go into the terminal.

"I know what she's supposed to look like!" she stresses. "Just do what I say do! She'll know us by the dandelion tattoo on my arm."

"Your what? You don't really *know her* know her? What about me? Does she know that you invited me on this damn trip and to let me slide on through, too?" Jack asks worried that he may be left out of the loop by old drug runner guy back in Jamaica who wants to sleep with his soon to be fiancée.

Candyce interrupts before Jack gets too loud. "Yes, yes, just hold my hand like you're doing now, and we both get through. Got it?" Candyce responds with her usual lackadaisical attitude while Jack stares at her in disbelief. Then, he finally speaks as thoughts of Candyce possibly deceiving him flow through his mind. He thinks of all kind of things such as her setting him up to take the fall so she can get back with her drug dealer guy back on the island. Even worse, paranoia creeps all over his skin causing him to become beet red with anger as he starts to truly believe in his heart that he could be getting set up for the worst fall ever if all the drugs are truly packed on his butt and not any actually on hers.

"Yeah," Jack takes a deep breath, trying to calm himself as he thinks about the ring he stole from the jewelry store in his pocket. "I got it," he continues to answer Candyce uneasily. He thinks so hard about the diamond ring that he can feel it literally banging up against the top of his thigh. Then, he stares down at Candyce's bigger breasts as she continues to grin and look around without a care in the world while he sweats bullets down his back. The thought enters his mind – are there really drugs inside her bra padding or is it just a fake way to make him carry all the drugs so she won't get busted? He looks at Candyce again like he could punch the hell out of her face, but calms down as he lets go of her hand. Then, he places his arm lovingly around her shoulders. "The girl with the light red tint in her hair, huh?"

"Yep," Candyce says adjusting her neck because Jack's arm is severely uncomfortable on it while she totes her bag. "But could you move your arm though? You know I don't like the feeling of someone's arm around me, locking me down."

"No, I can't remove my arm -not until we get right up where everyone can see us together, then I'll let go when we walk through security."

She snatches her body, but he holds her tighter. "Let go, Jack," she strains with the fakest smile on her face as the hairs on the back of her neck are starting to drip sweat, not because she's hot or nervous, but because his arm turning into a regular salt bath.

"No, no I won't let you go. If I go down, you go down."

"What?" She stops walking, but Jack continues, causing Candyce to drag along.

"You better come on if you don't want to end up in prison. You're probably trying to get me to go down as the scapegoat, huh? Play it off, remember?" Jack's face is beaming, all his pearly whites showing from ear to ear as he high steps down the walkway proud of the amount of control he has somehow grabbed in what could possibly be the last seconds of their vacation before prison. He takes deep breaths and even leans in for a kiss on Candyce's mouth that's already wide open in shock but still ready for the kill.

After she allows him to attack her face with a slob down, she, under her breath, blasts him, "Stupid ass. If we were going to get caught..." she starts, but he happily interrupts her.

"Shut up because here we go. There's your girl," he says, spotting the girl with the red streak in her hair. As he satisfactorily glances at Candyce, believing that he finally has her in his grip, he stops dead in his tracks when he looks back over at security. Candyce covers up his stall in gait by starting to cough to rule out suspicion because they are too close to security to start fidgeting. Jack catches on quickly and gives her pats on the back while whispering, "There are two fucking girls with red hair, Candyce. Two damn girls, not one, two!"

"There can't be, Jack," she whispers back and finally stands tall again to see what Jack sees. When she notices that he isn't lying, she simply removes his arm from her shoulders, grabs his hand, and continues to walk. "Fuck it and fuck you for that little stunt you pulled back there. He told me light red. I'll go with the lightest red hair I see. That's who I'll lock eyes with, and that will be our lady. Try some shit again, Jack, and I'll pull down your fucking pants right damn now and scream that you set my ass up. Now walk. Grow some balls."

"I could if you didn't pack..."

"Shh!"

Candyce notices one of the ladies with the red hair look down at her dandelion tattoo as she adjusts the strap to her bag while the other lady doesn't lift her head for a second wind as she inspects the bags of other passengers. The woman with the light red hair beckons Candyce and Jack over to where she is, passes them through the scanners which come out clean, and then she calls them over to pat them down. It's Candyce that moves over into location easily while Jack does so hesitantly, but Candyce can't concern herself with Jack as she allows the quick pat down. Once it's Jack's turn, he stands as tall and stiff as a stripper's pole, and when her hand runs down his buttocks, Candyce can tell that he sucks his cheeks in. That's when she spots the dogs, and her lungs collapse.

"Is there something the matter, ma'am?" Another agent comes to her side as her face turns pale. Not five seconds after, the agent with the dogs comes her way as Jack is freed to leave. Quick on his feet, he responds.

"She's pregnant. Do you have a quick bag or… we need the restroom," he states, staring hopefully at the woman who just sent them through. Jack moves Candyce over as the security guard with the light red hair walks directly in front of them to point them in the direction of the restrooms while giving them a random plastic bag. Candyce doesn't hesitate to grab the bag and move quickly, realizing that the agent just saved their lives before the dogs come sniffing.

"Just keep walking, baby. I'm sorry for what I did back there, but I need you to keep walking like you're about to really vomit. Spit some crap in the bag or something."

"I'm sorry. I'm so sorry. I saw the dogs and thought for a minute we had the wrong lady or those dogs were gonna smell…"

"Well, they didn't." Then he says loudly, "Come on, baby, we're almost there. Can you run?" His words are all a tactic to assume the future baby daddy role. When they turn the corner, the restroom is to the left, and even though Candyce feels better, she still plays her position. She goes inside while Jack stands at the door like a worried father to be when really, all the anxiety is coming from the hidden drugs.

"Oh my goodness! Oh my goodness!" Candyce pants over and over again as she gets as low as she can to the floor without touching it to see if anyone else is in the bathroom. When she sees it's empty, she immediately vomits into the sink and turns the water on full blast to pat her face down. Then, she checks her breasts and butt to make certain that everything is in place. Without another second's delay, she rinses out the sink and heads back out the door. Soon, they are on the outside of the airport, hungry, but not willing to go back inside. Candyce makes the call for their ride.

Chapter 9

I pull the bag of credit cards from the drawer and make a mad dash for my cell phone that continues to ring as the story of my life starts to unfold on television before my very eyes.

"Hello?" I ask, but I already know who it is. It's Candyce, and she's probably already at the airport waiting on me to come get her. As I sit on the couch with the credit cards on one side of me and the remote control on the other, I turn the television up louder so I can hear every word of the breaking news report that is being shot on the street where I live – Lincoln Avenue.

"Hey, Lisa, it's me Candyce. We're at the airport all ready to go. What's it gonna take you, like thirty minutes to get here or so?" When I don't respond, she speaks louder into my ear so I just say…

"Yeah, yeah, here I come. I'll be there in about thirty minutes like you said."

"Are you okay, girl," she laughs. "You sound like death."

I snap out of my daze for one second as the words of the news reporter become just one big major fog in my ears. "No, I just woke up. I'm on my way, okay? I'll come to the main parking area, but I'm not getting out. Just walk over there when I call. Bye." I don't wait on her to respond because I don't have to. I just know that I have to pick her up and fast.

"Right now, authorities are searching for a woman, possibly two, for questioning. Their names have not been released, but it seems that there has been a gruesome murder inside the home of 676 Lincoln Avenue. More details coming at…" I shut the television off, and my heart quakes as Smack comes and jumps up onto my lap to start licking my tears. I simply stand up with Smack in my arms. I rarely kiss a dog in the mouth, but this time, I kiss her like she's my own little baby. Looking down at her nose, I end up spotting a bit of blood from Robert's dead body on her hair, so I take her to the sink, gather some water in my hand and rub it out.

"There…there you are." I hold her into the air as she stares back at me, wiggling as if I'm her only friend in the world, and then I tell her, "Let's go get your mom." I have nowhere else to go. Walking past the couch, I snatch the bag of credit cards and ID's and head out the door fast, desiring to behave as normal as possible since so far, my name hasn't been released, but inside my body is a total wreck.

With each step I take to the car, my ears seem to fill up with wax because I forbid myself from hearing anyone who may call my name. My head is down and as my feet hit the pavement, I watch how my wet sneakers curve with my toes as they mush the street gravel. Even when I stick my key inside the car door, when the lock pops up, it looks so funny to me that I laugh, so I do it again. A flock of birds fly over my head, around in circles. There has to be about fifty of them, and they're all so free.

I stand there beginning to think about how everything in my life has changed all because of that whore in my bed and this damn black eye. Robert used to be my everything. Suddenly, his mom comes to mind and even his older brother and sisters, and my heart plummets even harder from the guilt of my killings causing them to suffer. Everything is so quiet…

"What the hell?" My thoughts are interrupted by something dropping on the top of my cataract sunglasses, so I rush into the car, toss Smack into the back seat, and grab them from my face as my fingers slide into something that feels creamy like melted butter. Immediately, I snatch my hands from my sunglasses as they tumble to the floor, revealing a white and black milky substance on the very top of the rim. Without an ounce of grace, I stare at my hands directly in front of my face completely mortified with the bird feces underneath my fingernails and running down my hand. I let out a huge scream in the car that catches Smack by surprise, and then I jump out of the car once again, slam the door, and return to the inside of Lug's apartment to wash my hands and sunglasses off.

"Stupid birds!" I shout with the front door wide open and just when I am getting ready to dry off and leave, there's a knock on the open door. My hands freeze onto the kitchen towel, and my hand reaches for the sharpest knife showing from the ajar kitchen drawer. Slowly but courageously, I look up at the doorway. "Oh hi," I respond to the familiar man knocking. It's Lug's friend, Jimmy Madison, from the neighboring apartment building.

"Hi," he stammers back. I glance at the television, and then back at Jimmy who is just standing there looking at me like I'm stealing something in my own flesh and blood brother's apartment when I have my own key to get both inside and out. It's him who hasn't been invited in yet. "Is Lug here?"

I step over to the edge of the counter, scooting the concealed knife along with me as it's wrapped up inside of the kitchen towel I was using to dry my hands. He knows something. I know this because usually when he sees me, he calls me by name really loudly in a jesting sort of way. For some reason today, he's seen a ghost and that ghost is me. "Come on in, Jimmy. He stepped out for a minute and told me to come over here. Have something to drink," I respond relaxed, taking a cup from the cabinet to fill it up with some cold water.

"Sure, yeah, I'll take some, Lisa," he says as he walks into the apartment. When he comes near, I reach over and grab the covered knife, scooting it closer to myself as I allow ice to fall into the cup from the fridge atop the water. Some of the water spills onto the floor due to me fixing the ice cold glass of water in reverse order, but it's okay. A little water won't hurt a soul.

"What have you been up to?" I ask walking to the edge of the kitchen counter again as I hold out my arm with the cup of water dangling from my bird poop free fingers. My left hand is still firmly atop the knife. He reaches for the drink, but instead of taking a sip, he continues to stare at my face.

"If you don't mind me asking, what happened..." he starts with his question as my heart begins to race. I squeeze the knife harder. "To your eye?"

"Oh my gosh, my eye! Oh that!" The adrenaline races through my body as I attempt to think of some raggedy excuse as to why my eye looks like the result of fifty broken black ink pens and a box of red melted crayons. "I fell...really hard against the edge of the countertop at my house."

"Is it gonna be okay? Are you okay?" he reaches out to touch it, and I jump back.

"Yeah," I grin hesitantly, "Of course, I'm ...or it's gonna be okay. First time for everything, right? It hurts like the devil, but..."

"But you can level with me, Lisa." He stares me square into my fucked up eye and then he looks into the other one. His build is of the husky type, with enough muscles to take down about two or three men with no problem. "No counter did that to your eye." He glances back at the television, and then picks up his cup to drink, placing it near his lips. "Especially when the news clip had your address on it." He turns back to face me and then cuts his eyes down at my body and then my hair before he begins to drink the water down. I was right. He knows something.

As he drinks, he sarcastically waits on me to respond as I watch Jimmy's huge Adam's apple go up and down with each swallow. I wait no longer, and the next time he slants his eyes at me while drinking from the cup, I squeeze the butcher knife in my left palm, raise it up while gravity pulls the kitchen towel downward to reveal the blade, and stab straight through his sarcastically, swallowing throat. "Sorry, Jimmy." And I keep stabbing because his big behind won't fall down. By the time I'm done, his throat is mangled, more water is on the floor along with him and blood, and I'm gone, locking Lug's apartment door behind me after rinsing off my hands. I come out fairly clean, besides a few spots, but my sunglasses are spotless.

Inside my Uncle Joe's car, I finally realize that things have gone out of control fast. My cell phone that sits on the passenger's seat has no missed calls although I'm expecting it to ring off the hook. Therefore, I shut it completely down, figuring that I will turn it back on only when I get to the airport. Wait, that's not the answer to my problems. I need to call Ma.

Turning my phone back on becomes a nightmare, but once it's back on and I'm at a standstill, I dial. The line starts to ring, and Ma picks up.

"Ma, hi," I start when she chimes in. My nerves riddle with panic as I wait in silence to find out whether or not she's seen the news broadcast preview clip before the real deal news comes on.

"Hey, baby," she drags, and my first thought is to explain. Before I open my mouth, she starts talking again. "Your Uncle Joe just walked in about five minutes ago, and he had a big cow about me letting you have the car to go pick up some friends to go, as he puts it, joy riding."

"Where is Uncle Joe now so I can talk to him about it?" I have nothing to say really except that I won't be bringing the car back anytime soon. Uncle Joe put so much work into this car. He only uses it for fancy dates and his own joy riding with Ma. He never really had nice things growing up is the story, so when he got enough money to buy what he considers a nice and good pair of running wheels, he went for it.

"He's outside having a smoke, and he's been stopped smoking, Lisa," she stresses. "When are you gonna have the car back so I can calm him down? I'm so tired of this."

Just then, I make up a good lie. "Eight o'clock. I'll have it back at eight. Look though, Ma. Whatever you do, don't tell anyone where I'm going…absolutely no one. Another thing. Keep the garage door closed. If someone comes asking about me, tell them I took the car earlier, but that's all you know."

There's a surrendering silence on the phone that pressures me to tell the complete truth, but I can't. In the background, I hear Ma moving quickly down the hallway. Her footsteps sound like thunder, and her breathing sounds like a mighty wind. By the way she slams the bathroom door behind her, which I know by the way it scrapes against the floor because it's off line, Ma isn't about to play games with me.

"Come again now, Lisa. You say you don't want me to say anything about you to anyone at anytime. What the hell is all this about? What the hell have you dragged me into?" she asks, as I hear the toilet seat go down.

Instead of responding to her question, I just keep driving. I can't tell her. I can't tell her I slit the bitch and her man, who was my husband, in my satined out sheets while Smack watched Robert beg for his cheating ass life. I can't tell her because I'm not sorry. I'm just not. They ate my food. They messed up my bed. He even gave me a black ass eye. Sure, I know I'm supposed to be sorry for what I did, but I'm just not. Staring into the rearview mirror at myself, I realize that I want to finally get away with doing something. I took the pain he gave me, and he didn't spend a night in prison for it… not one night. Now, just because I decide to fight back, the police are after me. Because some lady was in my bed, I have to go to jail because I gave her my pain. I'm dead now. Inside, I feel so dead, the same way I felt when I saw her with my Robert.

"Answer me, Lisa!"

"Ma!" I respond startled but clearly conscious now as I approach the interstate. "Just don't…"

"Just what the hell is going on here?" my Uncle Joe busts into the bathroom with Ma, and his voice is raging mad.

"I'm talking to Lisa is what's going on, and she's …"

"Hand me this phone," Uncle Joe shouts as I hear the phone drop to the floor, but before he picks it back up, I hang completely up on his angry ass. I can't do this right now.

"I love you, too, Uncle Joe." Sometimes he could be a pain, and today, he's doing it again. He can't just go with the flow. "Just this once, Uncle Joe, can you not be so aware of every damn thing!" I press on the gas, giving myself only fifteen minutes to get to the airport because I have a feeling, I'm running out of time. I don't even have a way to get any money because unless Robert put money in my account, I have none. My thoughts return back to his wallet that I should have snatched that sits on the bedroom dresser. I only have fifty dollars to my name and a half of a lottery ticket.

Chapter 10

"Hello? Hello, Lisa?" Joe commands as his wife looks on anxiously trying to figure out what's going on with both her niece, Lisa, and her husband as he holds the phone. Sure, he adores the car, but this is beyond what she's ever seen him behave in a while, especially against Lisa.

She snatches the phone from his hand. "Joe, what is your problem? She's bringing the car back. Now there isn't any need for busting through the door on me like a fool and jumping down her throat like a madman over a machine!"

"Oh yeah? Come on, Lyndi," he orders, grabbing her wrist and yanking it forward until she pulls away.

"Don't pull on me! What's wrong with you?"

"Come to this television right now! The news is about to start, and it's about Lisa."

Lyndi drops the phone onto the bathroom counter, and it accidentally falls into the empty sink. They both rush out into the living room where the news anchor has just started again with another short clip of what's to occur on the news at six. In the report is 676 Lincoln Avenue.

"Did you hear that, Lyndi? It's Lisa's address," he says, huffing and puffing like he just came back from a morning jog and forgot to pump himself full of water.

"Lincoln Avenue?"

He walks directly in front of her and places his hands atop her shoulders. "Yes! Lincoln Avenue!"

She slowly backs away and sits on the soft cushiony recliner that Joe bought for her years ago. Lyndi only sits in it when she has much on her mind and needs to relax. This is one of those times. As Lyndi takes her seat, she glances at the picture that sits on the sofa table of her and her deceased twin sister, Lisa's real mother, and weeps. All she remembers now is the promise she made to her sister - that she would take care of Lisa and Lug until she can't anymore.

Joe goes into the kitchen to put on some hot tea, Chamomile tea, which is known to be excellent for relaxation. When he peeps back in at Lyndi, he notices her crying, but he doesn't interrupt. His anger subsides as he is hopeful that everything is alright with the niece that he has grown to love as his own daughter. The tea pot goes off, and he steps over to pour the hot water into the teacups.

Joe is an older man, much older than Lyndi by about fifteen years. Age has taught him how to hold his peace and choose his battles. Now is the time to relax as much as possible. After finishing the tea, he takes one to Lyndi and then sits down on another chair. They both await the arrival of the news report as the coffee cools. Finally, the news anchor speaks.

"…today's breaking news comes from where our own news crew has gathered on Lincoln Avenue where, according to many witnesses, a female entered this home bloody and bruised and now is nowhere to be found. Sources have revealed that the woman in question, by the name of Lisa Caldwell, caught the attention of many shoppers at the grocery mart down the street when she went shopping in the store with blood covering her clothing and face. Shoppers say the woman seemed oblivious to the fact that she appeared the way that she did, and when she left the store, this is the home – 676 Lincoln Avenue – where she arrived. Brian, can you tell us more about what's going on currently near the home and what people are saying?"

"Well, Maria, I've questioned some of the neighbors who actually came outside of their homes from the commotion and some who literally watched whom they say is a woman by the name of Lisa Caldwell enter the garage of the home. They say that this home that you see behind me, is in fact the home where she resides with her husband. Unfortunately, there has been a murder, actually two murders, Maria, here at the home, but the woman seen entering the home is nowhere to be found."

"Brian, is she a suspect at this point?"

"Maria, they haven't said, however, right now they have said that they definitely want to speak with her as a person of interest and that's only because she may or may not be responsible for the killings that took place in the home. Officers say that she could have been forced and or even kidnapped or something of that nature, but those are just scenarios. The one thing they are leaning toward however is that this was a crime of passion, but they reserve to say to the public as of yet if she is the *only* suspect due to another car that doesn't belong to her that was found in the garage. It's that same car that has evidence of a crime inside it as well."

"Is there any idea about what possibly went on inside the home?"

"Yes, and it's pretty gruesome in fact. There are two people, a man and woman, who are stabbed to death. Of course, right now, no one is arrested, but the person of interest right now is Lisa Caldwell."

"Thank you, Brian. In other news…"

Joe turns the television off, and Lyndi slowly gets up to walk back to her niece's car that's parked inside the garage. Joe assumes his position and follows behind her carefully as not to send her off into a frenzy, but he already expects that things aren't going to be good. As Lyndi faces the hood of the car, she starts hesitantly toward the passenger's side door. The windows of the car she can't see through really well because she failed to turn on the garage light when she first walked inside. She turns back to look at Joe, however, and he flicks the light for her. That's when she turns to look inside the car. There are stains of blood soaked into her light gray upholstery. Lyndi quickly grabs her heart and falls against the wall.

"Joe! Joe!" she screams, as her heart completely breaks to pieces. "Not my niece, not my sister's baby. No, Lord, no God please!"

Joe comes to lighten her fall as he holds her from behind and pulls her back inside the house, shutting the door to the evidence behind him. The first chair they get to is at the door of the kitchen, and she slumps down onto it as Joe rubs her back. He knows that the only thing that stands between Lyndi's sanity and happiness is the future of her sister Linda's daughter which, as of now, doesn't look bright.

Chapter 11

"Since you're here, Luscious …Caldwell is your last name, right? I'm sorry, I left the note in the back with the rest of my things, and only remembered your first name well."

"Yes, it's Caldwell."

"Did I pronounce your first name right?"

"Sure did," Lug responds as he walks down the corridor with the new graduate lawyer.

"Good," she says relieved. As they continue walking, she assumes her roll as his mentor for the moment. "Well, since I was left sort of in charge of making sure you learn these halls fairly well for your first night…" She pauses at the first door at the end of the hallway. "This is where we break. Tonight, we probably won't even be in this room as we cram every single avenue we need to avoid and conquer for this case, but most times during the regular nine to five hours, we come in here to eat, chat, and release. Pretty nice, huh?" she asks.

Lug walks inside the room as she flicks on the lights. Ever since he had his first job as a bagger at a grocery store when he was a teen and throughout all his other ventures, he's never seen a fully carpeted break room, complete with sofas and chairs with center tables. There's even a huge balcony with seats for the taking.

"It sure is nice. Just this room alone looks one hundred times better than my apartment." He glances at her and then back at the room. "Yeah, my apartment can just about fit inside this area twice."

"Don't be so hard on yourself. Mine can fit inside it three times, but I'm not complaining."

"You serious?"

"Yeah, come on." She flicks the lights, and they walk out to continue the tour. "I just graduated not too long ago so between the student loans and all, I'm not quite there yet but thankful for all I have."

"I prefer to have much more than what I do have. That's why I jumped at this chance to work with you all, or at least shadow you on this case."

"Shadow? No way! By the time you get in there, we will definitely put you to work. We all have something to prove here in order to stay." She passes through the next door that allows them entry into the another. "Now this is the wide screen. Sometimes we all gather in here when there is a huge public trial to watch for training. At times, other graduate students are allowed to come as well just for the environment as extra bonus points for their classes. This room seats about fifty to seventy people, and watch…" She reaches over and grabs a remote control that sits atop a shelf. "This is one powerful HD television." She flicks it on and begins to flip through all the stations to stop on the news. "I wonder if I missed it."

"Missed what?" asks a curious and impressed Lug.

"There was some breaking news earlier, something about a murder that took place on Lincoln Avenue."

"Lincoln Avenue?"

"Yeah, and whoever it is that did it will no doubt make this law office one of their first stops to search for defense, that is if they have the money."

78

"Are you sure it was Lincoln Avenue?"

"Yep. Sure as...yep, yep. There it is at the bottom of the screen. 676 Lincoln Avenue. That's where the news clip said..."

Lug's mouth goes dry and his heart beats louder than the words the young, beginner lawyer is speaking. His palms start to sweat heavily, and he feels weak at the knees when he thinks about his older sister. Immediately he turns toward the door to head out, not thinking of this brand new interning opportunity with the firm.

"Wait, is something wrong, Luscious?"

"I need to make a phone call. I just...hold on, please. I'm sorry." Lug's voice cracks as he remembers just leaving his sister in the car, and now he hopes that he can just talk to her because he doesn't know if she's still alive, dead, or in trouble.

Chapter 12

As I drive down the road, the cars passing me by increase my paranoia. I'm thinking that someone, somewhere is going to identify me, and the time has ticked beyond when the news was to air. Therefore…damn. I glance down at my cell phone that sits inside the cup holder. It's Lug.

Hitting the steering wheel like a maniac as the traffic thickens, I continue to stare at the cell phone until it stops ringing. When I glance back up, the car in front of me slams on brakes. I veer to the right quickly, scraping Uncle Joe's car on the side as it pulls beside the guard rail, missing the other car. "Oh God," I swallow as I back up from the rail. The cars behind me are at a standstill. "It can't be that bad," I convince myself because I refuse to get out of the car to examine the damage. The phone starts ringing again, and it's Lug.

Up ahead is the exit that leads to the airport, and as the traffic begins to move again, instead of watching the cell phone down below, I sit it on the dash. It continues to ring, but I still don't answer. Lug is supposed to be at work, so that could only mean one thing – he has seen the news, and I'm on it.

"Stop calling me! Don't call me anymore." My nails dig into the steering wheel, and from the side of my eye, a little girl is waving her arm out of the window. I turn to her, but she isn't waving at me, but rather, she's waving at Smack who is running and jumping back and forth at the window behind me. There it is again. He won't stop calling, so I decide to answer it on speaker without saying a word.

"Lisa! Lisa, answer me. I swear to…Lisa!" After hearing the overwhelming agony in his voice, I decide to answer him.

"Hang up the phone, Lug. Go back to your work. Make a good life for us," I command him in the firmest voice that I can muster. I mean every word.

"What happened? I thought you were dead. They said people were dead at your house. It was your address, and it's all on television…it's everywhere and…"

"Lug! I'm not dead." I leave it at that. He can't possibly handle the truth right now, not right now. Therefore, I change the subject. "I dropped your bike off…put it inside your apartment. Where did you get all that stuff?"

"Lisa, where are you? Why are the cops at your house talking about people are murdered up in there? Answer me, dammit!" he strains, trying his best to keep his voice as muffled as possible.

"What are you doing with all those credit cards, Lug, and fake IDs? Tell me about that!"

"Did you kill somebody?" he whispers.

I don't answer. The less he knows, the better. At least he won't be able to lie to the cops when they come to question him like I know they will. Of course, he knows that they will question him as well, so it's better that I keep my mouth shut and drill him about what I found in his apartment.

"Who are you pretending to be, Lug? Somebody with a whole bunch of cash and credit or, I'm sorry, some people with a whole lot of credit cards? You're supposed to become a lawyer, Lug! A fuckin' lawyer!" I'm beyond pissed off because there was never a day, except today, that I would think he could potentially go to prison behind a lack of money.

"This ain't about me!" he yells, and just then, I hear a female's voice in the background. Lug ignores her and continues screaming into the telephone, "You're all I got! Tell me the truth! Just tell me, please," he weeps, and I can almost feel the tears trickling down his face. I ignore it anyway.

"I took that shit you had from the apartment. I'm gonna dump them after I cut them all up. You'll be fine...without me." I hang up the telephone as I hear him in the background screaming my name.

Chapter 13

"Where is she?"

"I don't know, Candyce! That's your best friend, not mine. Shouldn't she know that she should be here ahead of time?"

"What do you mean? I just called her, idiot. She can't just pop up in two seconds."

"I mean, doesn't she know we're hot?" he asks referring to the drugs on his both of their butt cheeks.

"Nope," she says rolling back and forth from the heel of her feet to her tip toes. "Nope she surely doesn't." Candyce's long, stringy blonde hair is blowing in the wind, and just before she looks inside her purse to pull out a cigarette, Jack grabs her arm.

"Excuse the hell out of me, Candyce? Come again?"

She leans over and kisses him on the cheek, and he glares at her. "Get your pale ass hands off my tanned ass wrist before we get thrown in a nasty ass prison because we smell like damn dope." He quickly removes his hand and she removes her cigarette from her purse. "We have to walk over here so I can smoke." She begins to trot along while Jack follows closely behind. "And no, just like you should have heard if your ears weren't so sealed shut, Lisa has no idea. She doesn't have to know because all she's going to do is pick us up in my car, drive back to her spot, and we'll continue on to our destination. We have to be there at eleven o'clock sharp, make the exchange, and it's just that simple. We're in the money for our part."

"Our part? Your part. I got me. As a matter of fact, since you're my woman, you got me. I don't know anything about this. As a matter of fact, when I get in the car, I will undress my ass back in the back seat and shove the shit in your bag."

"No you won't, so shut up. Stop being a thrill kill. You'll change at my house and then just," she continues, waving her hand at him like he's an annoying gnat, "follow me. You are such a bore. We're about to get paid, and you're acting like we got busted."

"No more traveling out of the country with you is all I have to say. I have enough problems to concern myself with..."

"Name one." She rolls her eyes and lights her cigarette.

"One what?"

"Problem. All you do is hang out with me, and then, when we're finished, you go back to work at the bowling alley."

The way he looks at her is with disbelief. If she could only imagine the trouble he's in if he gets caught with the stolen ring in his pocket. "You don't even realize." He finally pulls his jet black hair back, revealing his shaved scalp and loosens his pants a little bit. "Got me walking around here looking like a dork with dope on my ass. This is just..."

"You'll do anything for me, Jack. I love you, too," she smiles as a vehicle moves directly in front of them on the other side of the road. Jack notices it, however, Candyce is still looking back and forth for her silver Charger. The car's lights across the street flick on high beams, and Jack taps Candyce on the arm as she puts out her cigarette.

"Baby, look."

"At what? Damn, my shoes are scuffed. Dammit!" she complains lifting her foot up so that she can see the back of the shoe's heel clearly. "And then I stepped in some damn gum!"

"Candyce!"

"What?" she snaps.

"Who is this asshole flicking his lights at us? Is this another one of your people?"

Candyce stares across the street to try and figure out what Jack is talking about, but she has no idea who it is either. She grabs her cell phone, but doesn't move. Jack on the other hand gets paranoid and starts to back away.

"No, no," she grabs his wrist. "Don't move. You look guilty. Stand here with me and act normal. I'm gonna call Lisa to see how far away she is from us."

"Shit," he says under his breath.

"Well don't because you'll stink up the dope." She dials Lisa's phone, and on the first ring, she picks up. "Hello, Lisa, where are you?"

"It's me across the street. I've been trying to get your attention for the longest."

"Where's my car? I thought you were gonna pick me up in it so I could just drop you off and keep it moving. Now we have to unload and load and…" Candyce puts her on speaker phone.

"What's the big deal? A hello would be really nice right now, Candyce, and also a thank you. Just come on. This is my uncle's car. I was actually in it when you called me, and I wasn't going to ride back home to get your car." Lisa thinks fast. "Home to your place that is. It's inside your garage."

"You put it back at my place?"

"Yep, opened it with the remote and shut it back. Done deal." Lisa thinks even faster. "Robert came to get me when I dropped it."

"Oh. Well, thanks. Really," she responds, looking at Jack in a weird, stunned way. "Stay right there. We're coming now, as you can see." She flashes a smile and hops across the street with Jack trolling behind without a thing to say.

"Okay." Lisa hangs up the phone and watches them. With each step they take, her mind is on overload, thinking of any scenario to keep them from finding out her present and potential future. She needs money though, and Candyce just may be the right person to ask for it.

Candyce's parents are rich, but instead of rolling around in the doe, she rebels against it all. Her parents will give her anything she needs – cars, houses, big bank accounts – but she rejects it all because she thinks of them as way too high strung. It makes no sense, especially the part about her running away from home. She still wasn't broke when she did it. She had about fifty grand sitting there in the bank, and she blew right through it during her time prodigal. She hasn't been home since, and she likes it this way…living on the edge of nothing and the edge of something at the same time. Candyce has always been a risk taker, and Lisa believes that she does it all because she simply never appreciated the so called good life which Candyce swears isn't all that good.

When Jack approaches the driver's side window, Lisa nods at him and adjusts her cataract glasses. Then, she takes her newly sliced hair and tucks it behind her ears as best she can. Her hair has always been thick and her ears far too small to keep it back. She really did a full out wack job on it, and it looks superiorly unprofessional. Whatever the case may be, Lisa will think up another excuse to keep the ball rolling in her favor.

"Hey, girl! Thanks again for picking us up, and we hate to inconvenience you."

"Candyce, your tan is hot. People are going to mistake you for a sister like me...nice, brown and fine!" Lisa kids, but the joking emotion is nowhere to be felt inside her overrun-with-fear gut.

"Smack!" Candyce's baby girl hops into the front seat with her, and the licking begins. "Hey, baby! Did Auntie Lisa treat you right, huh, girl?" she mooches, and then her voice gets deeper. "Did Auntie Lisa treat that girl right?"

"She's alive, isn't she, Candyce?" Jack asks sarcastically. "Therefore, she's been taken care of just fine."

Candyce turns around and gives him a long, fifteen second stare, and that's when Lisa starts up the car because she's caught up in her own drama. "Are you constipated, Jack? Need a laxative, huh, boo? We just came off of a great vacation, and you're tending to trip heavily now that we're at home. Should I have left your tight ass there?" she asks in a high pitch. Jack doesn't answer. Then, Candyce turns back around.

"So, how was she? Greedy?"

"Girl, I hate when you make me watch Smack. She's cool and all, but she doesn't eat dog food from me…ever. Only the snacks."

"She ran out of the food I gave you?"

"Yep, but I got her something early this morning, some snacks, so she's fine."

"What have you been up to, and why *doth thou* have your uncle's ride. It's a nice car and all, but rather big for your taste, huh?" she inquires, adjusting her seatbelt. "Buckle up, Jack!" She then blows him a kiss which he doesn't catch. "And you really need to do something about those migraines…for real. I'm gonna talk to you about that medicine that can get rid of them for good, too."

Lisa rolls her eyes beneath the sunglasses. Candyce knows everything about Robert beating her in the face occasionally and how she keeps going back. What she has yet to find out about are the murders.

"I hear you, Candyce. I don't want to talk about that right now, though. Tell me about the trip."

"Superb! We had a blast, from the water to the hotel, which wasn't the absolute best, but it worked for us. Most of the day we were outside, and at night…" She takes a quick flirtatious glance at Jack who turns his head to look outside the window. "We did our thing underneath the trees. It was so romantic. Now, we're out of money, so it's back to work." She leans over into Lisa's ear. "I'll give you more of the scoop when we're alone. Jack is trippin' hard."

"Why?" Lisa whispers back, and Candyce shrugs her shoulders.

"Hormones I suppose. I guess he has something in his pants," she jokes, knowing that what she says is the full blown truth. Jack hears her, but is well aware of his girlfriend's sickening sarcastic ways.

He rubs on the diamond ring inside his pants' pocket, still hoping to give it to her when the atmosphere is right. Being this angry at her won't make for a grand proposal, and to top it off, she may even say no and he would have robbed the jewelry store for absolutely nothing. As he looks onto the highway that they are just now entering, he imagines the day when he can buy Candyce the world. No matter how much they argue, she is the only woman that he would even care to argue with. Jack is so in love with her.

Finally, they reach Candyce's neighborhood which is about five miles away from Lisa's residence. Everything is quiet in the small subdivision, and without blowing her cover, it's Lisa who is on edge with every press of the gas. She feels relief when Candyce opens her eyes from relaxing and speaks.

"I noticed your hair cut back there...and I wasn't going to say one word, promise to the heavens, but I can't just sit back and let it slide. Darling, who did it?"

"I did, Candyce. I just chopped it. I'm going to get it cut shorter tomorrow so I just thought I'd help her out. Actually, I wanted to see how I would look with it this short first, so I wacked it really quick." The lie comes out of Lisa's mouth so easily that Candyce buys it hook, line, and sinker.

"Well the length looks nice but the cut is a tragic sight." Suddenly, Candyce jumps up, her eyes big as apples. "Shh. Shhh!! Turn off the music! Stop this damn car."

"What?"

"Jack!"

"What? What?" Jack is looking around like someone is tailing them but finds no one.

"That's my house. Do you see that shit, Jack? Lisa, that's *my* house. What the hell are cops doing at my house?"

Between the trees and in between two other homes on the street, blue lights can be seen clearly parked outside of Candyce's house. In her front yard stands a tall Dogwood tree, and it can't be confused with any other tree because she's put pink bows all on it because pink happens to be her favorite color. She takes them off only in the winter to her neighbor's disgust.

"Oh shit. Oh shit!" Jack immediately puts his hands underneath his butt.

"Lisa, turn around. Turn around!" Candyce screams. "Go back to your place."

"What?" Lisa exclaims. Just as soon as the word exits her mouth, Lisa remembers Candyce's car. Traces of blood could have been found inside it in the garage that could have led the cops to her home. Then, she stalls the car in park, and turns to look at Candyce with unseen tears in her eyes because her sunglasses are on, but she strategically says nothing.

"Just go! Go somewhere, but do it now!" Candyce shouts.

"Okay, okay, okay," Lisa repeats as she pulls out of park from the side of the street. As soon as Lisa heads in the opposite direction which is back out of the neighborhood, Candyce and Jack duck their heads while Smack jumps back and forth between them. Immediately, Lisa's whole demeanor changes to a state of confusion, not knowing exactly why Candyce and Jack are hiding out. As far as she knows, she's the only one running from the law. She continues to drive, imagining the worst and refusing to say anything to Candyce about the murders she just committed less than twenty four hours ago.

"Just go to your house, Lisa."

"Man, shit, Candyce, I knew this shit would happen. I fuckin' knew it! Damn!" he hollers shoving his foot into Lisa's Uncle Joe's car door.

Lisa cringes at the sound of the car door being mangled, but says nothing. She turns right at the entrance of the neighborhood which results in Candyce going crazy.

"Lisa! That way! Get me off the streets!"

"Get you off the streets?" Lisa asks hysterically. "Why do I have to get you off the streets? You just got back from Jamaica!"

"We have drugs!"

"What!"

"And lots of it by the way. I'm up to my ass in dope," says Jack calmly from the back seat, but he really fumes with no place to go and release. He then punches the

91

seat with his fists, and with each blow, Lisa cringes until she finally yells.

"Enough!" Lisa's temper is about to erupt now, and she suddenly removes her cataract sunglasses, revealing her busted red eye that Robert so happily gave her hours before she stabbed him to death with the knife. Even though she hears the gasps of both Jack and Candyce with the reveal of her big, black eye, she grips the steering wheel as she drives, focusing on what may or may not lie ahead near the end of each street. There could potentially be road blocks to check each and every car that goes by, and there could even be someone that recognizes her or her uncle's car.

During the awkward silence, Lisa's phone starts to ring. Everyone in the vehicle looks down at it like it has the plague, but Lisa doesn't answer. She allows it to ring off the hook. It's Ma. Not only does Lisa allow it to continuously ring, but Ma continues to call over and over again. This is when she becomes nauseated; Ma knows everything that's going on.

"Please forgive me," Lisa mumbles to herself. The mumble is so faint that it is incomprehensible to her friends that are ducked down in their seats. Candyce finally asks her to pick up the telephone after the sixth call.

"Lisa, pick up the phone."

"I can't." She then looks at Jack in the rearview mirror and then back at the road. "It can be traced. It's a cell phone, remember. Turn it off for me. If they're looking for you, they might find me." She continues to drive, searching for the best escape route away from the prying eyes of people who have seen the news. Having no way of knowing what was shown or if her picture is flashing on television screens, she can only go with her gut. "Jack…"

"Yeah."

"I need you to go inside this motel up here at the exit and get a room. It should be no more than thirty dollars tops. Try to get a back room…say you need some sleep and you want to face the woods. When he gives you the room, we'll drive around…"

"Hell no. I can't do that shit," he responds to Lisa.

"Why not?" Candyce interjects. "Jack, they're at my house! We haven't even seen the news. My picture might be up everywhere, so I can't go inside at all."

"Well, why can't she go?" questions Jack in reference to Lisa. "Nobody's looking for her. It makes perfect sense."

Candyce stares over at Lisa who hears every piece of logical theory that Jack has suggested, but she is now thinking of the best way to make what he said illogical or dangerous. The fact of the matter is that the cops could either be at Candyce's house for the drugs or, which makes more sense, they could be at her house because she's become suspect in a double murder – murders that she didn't even commit. Therefore, Lisa blurts out the first thing that comes to mind.

"This is my uncle's car."

"And?"

"And I'm in charge of this vehicle, plus…" Lisa responds to Jack's sarcastic remark, "I'm flat broke. I have no money. Well, not enough."

"You don't have…" Jack states furiously. "Here! Here, take the money and the car keys with you. We don't want this as a getaway car!" Then his voice raises to a piercing squeal, "This is so freaking dumb ass! I wish I never got in the car with you two in my whole fuckin' life, I swear! Just get the room, get back in the car and drive around to the room. Makes perfect sense to my heated ass. Does it to you, Candyce?"

"Don't talk to Lisa like that and me either, okay, Jack! It's not her fault we're in this shit anyway."

Lisa simply stares straight ahead, dismissing the comment as possible, however.

"Say that one more time, Candyce!" He leans over and plants a huge kiss on the side of Lisa's face and then forces himself back down in the backseat. "I'm so sorry, Lisa." He then points at the woman with whom he is slowly falling out of love. "Send her ass inside because she got us in the damn mess! All I know," he argues, pointing at his chest and pushing his hair from his face, "is that I'm not getting out of this car unless I have somewhere to hide my head, dammit."

"Jack!" Candyce screams, "You're such an asshole!"

"I'll go!" Lisa finally gives in, honestly believing that it's her own indiscretions that got Candyce tied up in this trouble in the first place, regardless of their drugs.

"Are you sure?" Candyce asks terribly frightened for her friend who may end up an accessory to their crime.

"Yes…yeah. I'll go." The motel's lot isn't that full, so Lisa pulls into a park that is far enough away from the entrance that the attendants can't see the car. Before getting out, she puts on her sunglasses and pulls down her visor. "Check around for cameras because if we're in their line of vision, we have to pull out of here and try another motel."

"There's one right there, but it's pointing at the rooms and not the lot."

"Did it get us when we came in?"

"No way. It's not moving. Candyce, you see any?"

"No…uhm uhm. I don't see any on this side. There is one over there at the entrance though. Here, wear my hat just in case. Everyone knows you're my best friend. If they see you, then they see me and vice versa."

"Yeah…yeah." Lisa agrees.

"No, no, this is all wrong. Look at her. She looks suspect, Candyce. Those big ass glasses on and your wide brim? This is all about appearance. Give me your brush so I can lay my hair down. I'm going in."

"You are?"

"Yes. Meet me at the back. If I'm not back there in ten minutes, break out. There's no line in there at all, so I should be in and out. Let me have that change back, Lisa."

She hands him the money back, and he gets ready to serve up another act that may cost him his life. Although he's mad at the situation, he can't get it out of his head that the cops may really be at Candyce's house for him and jewelry heist, not the drugs at all.

The bell sounds off at the front entrance as Jack walks with his head down pretending like he's fixing his watch when in reality, he's hiding his face from the cameras. When he reaches the front desk, a very petite attendant is fiddling with her hair, but when she notices Jack, she pulls herself together and greets him.

"May I get you a room for tonight?" She blows a pink bubble with the bubble gum that's wrapped around her tongue. As she looks into her computer, paying attention to Jack is the last thing on her mind. Jack notices her greet-yet-ignore the customer attitude and loves it.

"A room at the back...I need some sleep," he yawns, placing his elbow on the counter with his eyes closed. "Keep the sun out of my eyes for some hours or so."

"I understand that. It's much cooler at night at the back as well since the sun sets over here. Let's go with room number forty-five. It's around back and dead center of the motel. Thirty dollars for a night, and you can have the key. Bring it back to me when you check out at or before eleven o'clock tomorrow, sir. Just fill this out and you're on your way."

"Thanks." Jack holds his breath as he takes the pad and pen thinking that she will ask for identification. Until she does, however, he fills out a wrong name along with other fraudulent information to get him by. Today is his lucky day. The attendant doesn't request he show ID. From there, he hands her the paper and money, takes the key, and heads toward the exit, playing with his watch again on the way out.

As he reaches to open the glass door, another person is coming inside, so he immediately steps to the side and pretends to scratch an itch on his ankle so they won't waste time being nice by holding the door open. When the feet walk past him, he continues on out, not even looking at Candyce and Lisa as he strolls pass the car. Candyce looks back at him for some sort of sign while Lisa keeps her head down. That's when Candyce's cell phone rings. It's Jack, and she picks up.

"Room forty-five." He hangs up the phone.

Candyce quickly glances at Lisa. "He's going to room forty-five. Let's pull out."

Lisa puts the car in reverse and drives past Jack as he walks differently than usual. He's sloping his shoulder down and walking like someone who has a disability or a severely crooked spine. Candyce notices his gait as well, and asks, "What the hell?"

Instead of trying to figure it out, Lisa decides that she could care less and turns the corner while she watches through the rear view mirror as Jack walks inside the corridor to get to the back of the motel. The car gets back to the other side before he does, so they see him step out and look side to side for which way to turn to get to the room. It's to his right. Lisa spots the room before anyone and turns into the parking space. Candyce watches as Jack opens the door, and then, leaves it open. Then, she grabs Smack, hops out of the car along with Lisa, and they both bolt inside.

Chapter 14

When Lug comes back around the corner, his new associate is standing there looking at him like she's seeing a ghost, even worse, someone that's in really big trouble. His cell phone feels like it's thumping inside his hand, so he shoves it deeply into his pocket and straightens himself out the best he can as he stands before his temporary trainer with tears in his eyes.

She doesn't know what to say as she looks back at Lug because she barely knows him, but she pushes through all her hesitation and tells him, "Whatever it is, it's going to be alright."

Lug stares back at her and agrees, "I know. I know that. It's nothing," he sniffles although his happiness about the new internship and income is down the tubes now that his sister is in some sort of trouble. On top of that, his own secret has been blown about his credit cards. He needs at least one of those cards in order to get his car fixed and pay his rent because he's totally broke and has nothing to sell for it.

Sorrowfully, he looks around at the intricate detail of the wallpaper of the firm's walls, and then his eyes fall back toward the young lady who stands in front of him, on the good side of the law. Lug knows he's stuck in the middle of both the good and the bad, if there is such a thing. He clears his throat and then speaks.

"I have to go. I really don't think that I can stay here…not today. I can't explain."

"She's related to you, isn't she?"

Lug's thoughts plunge to the ground at the thought of everyone finding out that the person making the news right now is his sister. They're all lawyers, not idiots, therefore, they figure things out just as well as he does without half of the details being revealed on the television; those details being that the woman named Lisa Caldwell possibly has much to do with what has happened on Lincoln Street.

Lug reaches out to her and places his hand atop her shoulder. "Please don't say anything about this. I don't know anyone here yet, so please, just say…"

"You got sick." She moves her shoulder from underneath his hand. "You did get sick, and you had to leave." Then, she puts out her hand to shake his. "Don't worry. I got you. My family used to stay on the news. I understand when you don't want something to get out."

Lug shakes her hand with both of his. "Thank you."

"You have my word."

"Thank you! Thank you so much. I need to get back to my place and…"

"Take my car," she offers abruptly, "since you said back there you had to be dropped off. You can't be that bad a guy right? Just bring it back. Here is my number. I'll keep an ear out for what I hear about…"

Lug stalls with talking anymore than he already has. Who he sees as an innocent young lady trying to help may be just the opposite. He's not accustomed to any strange woman being as helpful as she is being to him, especially with him being brand new to the firm and all. Therefore, he passes on her suggestion.

"An ear out about what?" he asks with a deep sense of paranoia overtaking him.

"About who you were talking to on the phone."

"And who was that?"

The young lady pauses and takes a step backwards, intimidated by his line of forgetfulness and questions. "Well, I'll just see you another day. I'll tell…"

"No, I have his number. I'll tell him…right now," he says matter of factly, and while she stands in front of him, he dials. When the person in charge, Mr. Donalds, picks up, Lug begins to speak on speaker phone. "Hello, how are you doing, sir. This is Luscious, Luscious," He glances up into the young woman's eyes. "…Caldwell. I just got really sick to my stomach in the bathroom here at the firm, and I may be coming down with the stomach flu or something that I don't want to pass to the others. I need to take at least twenty-four hours until this passes out of my system if I may do so."

Lug places the phone up to her ear and grits his teeth together for her to agree. Without much delay, she does what she feels he wants her to do.

"Yes, yes sir. He nearly did it all over the floor, so it would probably be best that he rest tonight."

"Say no more, Luscious. You're free to go. Call up in the morning just in case."

"Thank you, Mr. Donalds." They hang up the phone and Luscious walks right past her as she desires desperately to take back the lie that has already sailed from her lips by her own free will. As he continues down the hallway, tears begin to well up in his eyes once again as he thinks about his deceased mother and the high hopes and dreams she had for them, and he apologizes. "Mom, I'm so sorry. I'm so, so sorry." When he finally exits the firm, he leans on the brick wall and calls an ex-girlfriend for a ride back to his apartment.

Chapter 15

"Just find the damn remote control, Jack!"

"I'm looking! Can't you see that? What kind of motel is this where the remote control isn't in plain view?"

Lisa locates the remote control on the floor and flicks on the television while Candyce takes every jab at Jack that she possibly can. Jack gets up from looking underneath the bed when he hears the television come on.

"Next time, could you say something, like *I found it*?" he says to Lisa who ignores his bitter mood. She has more important things to worry about.

As she flips the channels, not one channel is playing the news. The next time the news will come back on is at ten o'clock sharp, and by that time, she wants to be long gone from the motel room that smells like rotten five day old sex.

"This room stinks," Lisa complains.

"Tell me about it," Candyce responds, "But we have no choice. I still have to get this dope delivered for my cash on time, cops or no cops."

"Where is the dope again?" Lisa asks.

"On my ass…and Jack's ass, too."

Lisa goes quiet from all her questions only for a couple of seconds, and then asks, "But you didn't get caught at customs, so why would the cops be there for you now?"

Candyce hears her question, but chooses to ponder over it instead of answering it right away. She fiddles with her hair a little bit, and even gives herself a foot massage while Jack goes into the bathroom to relieve himself of the solid stuff and not the liquid. Then, she looks back at Lisa who is just sitting on the edge of the bed, quietly as Smack runs around the room sniffing for a place to poop.

"You know what? You're right. Why would they be at my house unless someone snitched?" Suddenly, she jumps off the chair and dives onto the bed next to Lisa. She grabs her by the arms and whispers into her ear. "You think it was Jack?"

"What?"

"Jack!" she whispers, pointing wildly at the bathroom door that has a foul odor seeping from underneath it. "Who else would it be, Lisa? No one else knows where I live or what I do, and no one else would turn my ass in that's in the game with me!" She punches the mattress. "Bullcrap, it has to be him, so let's leave his ass now!"

Lisa stares back into the eyes of her girlfriend who is gone completely manic. She's moving through the room a mile a minute. Telling Candyce about the whole murder is on the tip of her tongue, but still, she keeps quiet about it. It's one of the only things she's ever kept from her since they've been friends. Finally, Lisa interrupts Candyce's fidgeting with a comment.

"I don't think it was him. It just doesn't make sense, but Candyce..." she pauses.

"Yeah?"

"Just what the hell are you doing drug trafficking anyway? Your family is rich as hell, so why are you doing this? For what? You were just gonna have me come pick you up and drop you off and surprise!"

"You were never supposed to know. Ever. That was supposed to be the last time," Candyce whimpers, grabbing her hands. "I'm so sorry, and I didn't want you involved. I don't know how the cops ended up at my house, and you could have gotten arrested with me and... I just have absolutely no idea what's up right now."

"It's okay."

"Really?"

"Yeah." Lisa turns to the motel room door. "People make mistakes all the time. I would want you to forgive me for my wrongs, just like I want God to forgive me for anything I've done wrong. So yeah," she continues, turning back to Candyce who is just about on her knees, "you don't have to beg me. I know what it is to make a split or planned decision. The question is how do we get the drugs off of you quickly..." Lisa pauses abruptly, feeling the need to explain her understanding attitude that comes with a financially stable ulterior motive.. "It's just that you're my friend, and friends...we help each other...no matter what. I can't have you going to prison, not over this." Lisa gets up from the bed, cutting her eyes backward at Candyce. "I'll just take you to deliver the dope. How much money will you get?"she asks, pretending to be more in awe that Candyce is making money the illegal way.

"About twenty grand. Lisa, thank you so much. I'll even give you five. I love you!" She jumps up and gives

Lisa a big hug. "If I don't deliver this dope, I don't know what or who will be after me for it."

Lisa grabs her right back and says, "That's what friends are for."

Jack comes out of the bathroom and watches his girlfriend in an embrace with Lisa. He then shakes his head and says, "The toilet's broken." Then he tosses his deeply padded underwear on the bed. "Where do you want me to put your other half of this stash?"

Chapter 16

"If you need me for anything else, Lug, just let me know. When you talk to your sister, let her know that she's in my prayers."

"I will, Shy-Anne. I will. I just don't know what's going on, and I don't even know where she is right now. I just got this job, well this internship, at the firm that actually pays so I can stay on my feet." Lug opens the car door, but before he gets out, his ex-girlfriend Shy-Anne grabs his hand.

"Everything is going to be okay. Are you sure you don't want me to come in?"

"No, no, I'm good." He leans over and gives her a peck on the cheek. "I just need to be alone right now until I can talk to her, wherever she is. It doesn't look good, though, Shy."

"Well, I'm off work, and Mia is at her grandmother's so that I can get some rest until my work week kicks in again. Call me. Let me know what's up. Just because we aren't together anymore doesn't mean I don't still care about you as a friend."

"I got you. See you around. I'll call you, and tell Mia I say hi."

"Will do." She backs up the car after Lug makes it to his door, and he watches her as she drives off as the day turns into night. He turns back around to stick his key into the door, and that's when a friend comes around the corner, calling his name.

"Lug! Wait a minute, Lug. Have you seen Jimmy? He told me that he was going over to your place earlier to ask you about something, and he's not back yet. I've been asleep, getting ready for the night shift I have to pull at my new job, and I want to make a good impression. I can't bring this baby into the world without any money," she says pointing at her yet-to-conform-to-roundness womb.

"No, I haven't seen him. I'm just now getting back home from my job. He was here?"

"Yeah, I guess," Jimmy's fiancée, Raigen, replies. "He never came back home."

"No, sis. He's not here. Like I said, I'm just getting back."

"Yeah, I know. I saw you out the window, and that's why I ran out to catch you. This is weird," she continues, spinning around on the sidewalk confused about why she isn't seeing Jimmy. "Okay then," she turns to walk away, puzzled. "Well, if you see him or talk to him, let me know. I'm getting worried. He doesn't do this...ever. I wanted to say good-bye to him before I left so I could have good luck tonight on this gig."

"I'll let you know, and if I see him, I'll send him home to you."

"Thanks!" She jogs back around to her apartment, and Lug opens his apartment door. Immediately, he sees his bike on the wall, so as he closes the door behind him, he lifts it up high, placing it on the hook he has for it that's attached to the front door. From there, he looks at his cell phone, sees nothing, and then turns around to walk toward the bedroom, but on his way there…

"Oh, Jesus!" He stumbles over to his television, hitting the shelf so hard that it causes the television to wobble. His hand covers his mouth and through his fingers comes the vomit. There, lying on the carpet, is Jimmy, starring at the front door with his throat gashed open from one end to the other.

"Oh God, oh no God, oh, Jesus, help me," he calls, falling to the floor as he grabs his Bible from the bottom of the shelf, placing it against his chest. "Please, Lord, don't let this be real," he pleads, closing his eyes and praying continuously. He immediately becomes sick at the stomach again, and vomit smears all over the carpet as he puts the Bible down and slides slowly toward the dead man he knows as Jimmy. He looks at the front door, contemplating running back to Jimmy's fiancée, but that would mean him catching a sure prison sentence.

"I didn't do it. I didn't..."

His eyes grow wide, and he slams his body against the wall, unwilling to go anywhere near Jimmy although Jimmy's eyes seem to be staring right at him. Lug scoots himself into the tightest position he can and dials his sister.

"You have reached..." says the answering machine.

"Dammit!" Lug exclaims as he starts to vigorously clean his hands off on the carpet. Then, he slides up the wall, keeping himself as far away as he can from the dead and bloody body lying on the floor. The kitchen and the dining room are adjacent to one another, only separated by a portion of the kitchen counter. Therefore, he walks into the dining area, reaches over into the kitchen, and turns on the water at the sink to wash off his hands thoroughly.

The drawer that held fake credit cards and identification cards is halfway open, and Lug can tell that all of what he needed to make one more merchandise sale for the rent is gone. He doesn't care though because there's no way he can come back to the apartment. He looks around, but he stands at a loss with only one thing to do – cross over Jimmy's dead body to get into his room, grab a few things in his book bag and go.

Chapter 17

All three of them look at the dope that's sitting on the motel bed. That's when Candyce looks back at Jack with a suspicious eye.

"What?" Jack asks with much attitude. "It's your dope!"

"Did you snitch me out? How would they know to be at my house and we didn't get pulled by customs, huh? Tell me that? Jack," she continues, walking away from a quiet Lisa toward her boyfriend. "You're the only other person who knew what I was gonna do in Jamaica."

"Are you serious?" Jack spins around in the room about three times, each time stopping to stare both Candyce and then Lisa in the face. He laughs hysterically the whole time, but on the last spin, he stops with a completely different appearance on his face. This time, it's a look of nervousness. "No, no...I didn't rat on us, Candyce," he says somberly. Then, he sits on the bed slowly, hesitating to look back up into her eyes. He feels cornered, so he gives in, ready to fess up to the other reason why the cops may be at her doorstep. "They, well, the cops...they could have been looking for me...but it's not likely..."

"What? What! You!" Candyce swings her head Lisa's way, and then back at Jack. She does this a total of four times as her blonde hair soars in the air from shoulder to shoulder. "Just what in the hell fire did you do so damn wrong that the cops came to my house?" She throws her hands up in the air and turns back to face him with an expression that reads I could kill you. "And now you tell me! Now, Jack. You stupid f..."

110

Quickly, Jack ducks as Candyce swings toward his face. She misses, and he then shoves his hand into his pocket while the other hand blocks Candyce's second attempted attack on him. All Lisa does is watch, too consumed with her own hidden crimes that top the dope hands down. She is interested in everything the two have to say, however, so that she may be able to continue her silence and have the upper hand.

"Look, look! I'm sorry alright," he yells, shoving the diamond ring directly in between her eyes. She backs up and her mouth falls completely open as she inspects the diamond. "I wanted...want to marry you. Look," he continues getting down on one knee and moving his hair out of his face. "I know we argue all the time and have gotten ourselves into some dumb shit, but we can make it through. I'm asking you to forget all my cussing and blaming you for everything that's been going on for the last couple of days. Will you marry me, Candyce?"

Candyce's face turns redder than a strawberry as she reaches for the diamond ring with her fingers that are now shaking like someone who just downed some dope. When she grabs it, she scopes the diamond like she's a professional jeweler, and then she looks back into her boyfriend's eyes. He stands to his feet before her and speaks.

"I was supposed to give it to you in Jamaica, but when you told me about this drug trafficking and how you wanted me to help, and...I just got pissed because I'd already risked my life getting this for you because I know, without all this drug stuff, you are the woman I want to spend the rest of my life with."

Candyce's eyes flow tears, and she steps two feet away from him. "What do you mean you risked your life for this?"

He looks up at Lisa who is staring back at him, trying not to miss a word, and then he leans back in toward Candyce and whispers something in her ear. Whatever he whispers causes Candyce's chest to go up and down, almost to a state of hyperventilation. She then turns to Lisa who hasn't turned from them at all, although she can feel that Jack may want some sort of privacy in the tiny motel room. She certainly isn't going into the bathroom where there's a broken toilet that is still seeping out a pungent odor that overshadows his heartfelt proposal.

As Jack and Lisa stand there awaiting Candyce's response, she erupts into laughter and then leaps onto his chest. Because he wasn't ready for the dive, he falls backwards onto the bed while she kisses him all over his face. The cocaine that Jack took off his behind only minutes ago when he broke the toilet, catches Candyce's attention, and then she jumps up off the bed.

"What?" Jack asks.

"Take this off me. Take it off! I don't want cocaine covering me when you ask the second time." She snatches off her clothes as fast as she can, and while this whole fiasco is going on, Lisa stands there in the same spot looking totally confused as Smack jumps onto the bed. Finally, Lisa snaps out of it when Candyce calls her over.

"Come here…move, Jack! Move, Smack! Come here, Lisa. Fix me up. Jack, turn around and here, hold the ring again."

Lisa quickly takes about three steps to reach her ecstatic friend who is literally butt naked, tossing the rest of the drugs from her bust and bottom over onto the bed. Then she puts her clothing back on while Lisa brushes her long, stringy hair.

"You know I don't do Caucasian hair well."

"Well, so...just brush it. I want you to be as much a part of this as I am. I'm so excited. Turn around, Jack!" she yells, flicking her hands at him. Then, she whispers to Lisa, "If it wasn't so stink in the bathroom we could fix me up in there. And guess what? He is the guy from the Orlando jewelry heist! I didn't even know!"

Lisa ignores the whole bathroom thought, but her gut drops to her feet when those words of the heist come sailing from Candyce's lips. Lisa simply takes several deep breaths to remain calm as the news of her hanging out with soon to be felons sinks in, along with the fact that she's about to be one herself. The sooner she leaves, the better.

"There you are," she tells Candyce after flicking her hair to the left and right a bit. It's so stringy that there's absolutely no fluff to it at all, so Lisa just cracks a smile and hopes for the best with the second proposal. "You're all set." There's a digital alarm clock on the small desk by the bed that Lisa continues to glace at while Candyce tells Jack to turn around.

"I'm ready!" Candyce stands on her tip toes while Jack turns around with the ring and gets back on one knee. Lisa moves back to her original position and takes a deep breath when she hears a sound at the motel room door. It's feet shuffling around at the entrance, and while Jack babbles, she tunes him out so that she can try and hear what the fumbling is all about. Slowly she creeps toward the window.

"Lisa!" She points down at Jack's face that is looking up into hers. "Look!" she squeals.

Lisa just smiles, gets a better look outside through a split in the curtain and then turns back to face Candyce in her big moment. To Lisa's gratefulness, there are only three drunk guys stumbling to their room. By the time her concentration is back onto Jack and Candyce, the re-proposal is all over and done.

Jack stands back up, tall and strong, feeling good about this one, small moment in time that happens to fall in between such devilment. They stand there kissing which leads Lisa back into memories of her lost love. Slowly, she slides down into the chair, and as she watches them, she recalls the minutes it took her and Robert to complete the marriage kiss of a lifetime.

As they stood in a beautified church yard full of people and a large canopy, it was all Lisa could do to contain herself from the man of her dreams. They'd already recited their vows to one another and even giggled a little as the crowd watched. Her gown was fitted with a train that flowed around her feet, and Robert's shoulders looked massive in his dapper tux that smelled of the cologne she bought him. Lisa was so in love with everything about Robert. His eyes and his lips were perfect. There was nothing more that she wanted than to have plenty babies with him and live happily ever after in his arms. That all changed after the first hit which was a mistake. They were arguing about many things but the main thing was her not getting pregnant. Robert hit her as he turned around swinging his arms, at least that's how Lisa saw it in her mind. That's when she let the incident go, and after that, she began to let more and more of herself go until she lost all of who she was for him, just to make him happy. The fists continued, and she proceeded to lose herself until that last hit brought her back beyond her senses. She killed him.

"Girl, wake up!"

Lisa snaps out of it. "I'm just tired. I need to get back home," she says obviously lying but not to their knowledge.

"Yeah, I know but do us this favor, and I promise you won't regret it. Take us to the spot. I'm gonna call my connect so he can meet with us early. That sounds fair, right? I'll let him know that you're coming as well, but they're gonna hose you down."

"What?"

"They have to hose you down because they don't know if you're a cop."

"Candyce!"

"Please! There is money in it for you. I promise. I've known him for a very, long time, so believe me when I tell you, he may be dangerous but he won't hurt me unless I hurt him. So far, I've delivered."

Lisa ponders over the many scenarios of how things can go down, and she quickly accepts the fact that she has a better chance with them than without them. Besides, Candyce holds all the cards because she's getting all the money. She then eyes the newly engaged and loving it Candyce and tells her to...

"Make the phone call."

"Just call Robert and tell him that you're gonna be a little late. Tell him my flight isn't in yet." She hits her phone. "If we had free Wi-Fi in this dump, I could check the news from my phone." She sits on the bed and Lisa immediately jumps up.

"Yeah, no Wi-Fi, so is this all the dope?" Lisa asks nervously. She totally forgot about the internet.

"Oh, yeah. Hold on." Candyce waits on the phone to ring, and when it does, she takes it off speaker, gets up from the bed, walks toward the bathroom but makes a U-turn and goes back to the bed to talk to who is believed to be her contact. "Hi, listen, it's me, Candyce. I'm back so I need to stop by to see you about ten o'clock instead of eleven. My car caught a flat," she lies, "so one of my girls came to get me. She's good. She's my best friend and she doesn't know one thing. She...her name is Lisa. She's gonna swing me by the spot and you'll have a gift for your girl. Is that alright?" She pauses to listen, and then speaks. "So you are having a water balloon party? Do we have to wear bathing suits, I mean, is it necessary?" Candyce's face drops, however, she responds cheerfully, "Great! See you at ten!"

Jack taps her repeatedly on the shoulder, and Lisa slumps over even further. By the end of the conversation, it's known that water will be thrown and the time is rearranged. Ten o'clock sharp is the drop.

Chapter 18

"Hello, hello? Hello, Aunt Lyndi?" Lug answers his phone. He's already jumped Jimmy's dead body to get into his bedroom to grab some underwear, his toothbrush and paste, along with a pair of jeans and three shirts to stuff in his book bag. He looks at his law school books that he has taken good care of since he's had to scrape by to make it this far in his career, and he immediately gets sad. Although the phone is up to his ear, he can't hear anyone talking. "Aunt Lyndi?"

"Hi, baby. Oh Lord," she cries aloud. She sounds as if she's lost her only child. "Lug, sweetheart, are you okay?"

Lug pretends like he doesn't know what's going on while he stares at Jimmy's dead body only feet from his own feet. Jimmy's right arm is twisted awkwardly on the floor with his fingers outstretched like he was in the struggle of his life before he died. As he stares, his aunt cries, not able to get the words out, so his Uncle Joe gets on the telephone.

"Lug, nephew, how are you doing, man?"

"I'm fine...I'm good." he lies as he finishes zipping his book bag. Afraid to ask but willing to do so anyway, he continues, "What's wrong with Aunt Lyndi?"

"I think you need to come over here, Lug."

"I don't have any way to get over there. My car needs to go in the shop. All I have is my bike and..."

"Well then sit down." Uncle Joe takes a deep groan into the speaker of the phone, and Lug's knees weaken because he still doesn't know the full story. "There's been some killing at your sister's house. I don't know if you've seen the news or not, but it doesn't look good."

"A murder?" Lug thinks about leaving out the fact that he saw Lisa today, but he decides not to go that route. "Who was killed? I just saw Lisa. She dropped me off at work in your car, unc!" he answers, trying his best to sound as if he has no idea what happened. Jimmy's dead body is extremely distracting, so he turns to face his dresser. That doesn't help because he ends up looking at Jimmy's dead body as a reflection in the mirror, so he moves over to his bedroom window.

"She did?" his uncle asks concerned. "Did she say anything to you out of the ordinary?"

"No...she cut her hair and all but that's it." Lug's voice quivers but he removes his head from the phone until he quickly gets it together. "She just told me that she was going to pick up some friends."

"Well, your aunt said that your sister came by, and she uh...said that she'd just finished babysitting some kids that soaked her wet. Then she got some of your aunt's clothes, she left her car saying, just like you said, that she needed to get some people from the airport. Her hair was cut and all, but uh... We just watched the news report, and after it said that people were murdered, Lyndi got up to look inside Lisa's car. It's parked in the garage there... It has what looks like blood in it, Lug." His uncle chokes up. "I haven't called anyone but you because her car...I don't...I'm not ready for the cops to arrest her yet, me nor your aunt. They don't even know her car is here, Lug."

"Her car is there...bloody?" Lug nearly faints. "Hold on, Unc." He places the phone down and takes a couple of deep breaths. His thoughts travel to his sister going to prison for life because contrary to what he wants to believe, Lisa may have killed not only some people at her house, but also the dead man on his floor. Finally, he raises the phone, having thought of a way to keep his aunt and uncle away from cops for some hours in case they come knocking. "Just pretend like you all didn't see the news. Get out of the house. Go to a movie. If you are out of sight, you should get no questions. Let me find out where Lisa is so I can talk to her." Then he pauses. "I don't believe she did that, Unc. Tell Aunt Lyndi that Lisa's innocent. It was somebody else."

"She's driving my car, Lug. The cops…"

"Just leave the house, Unc. Go out to eat in the other car! Just let me think. Love you, guys. Things are gonna be alright. Tell Aunt Lyndi that it's okay."

"Lug?"

"Yeah," he answers, sniffing and wiping his eyes, already starting to toss things around in the room looking for an extra credit card and maybe even some identification.

"Don't put yourself in jeopardy trying to save your sister. I know you love her, but…"

Lug hangs up the phone. He doesn't even consider what his uncle was saying about helping his sister if he can. The fact is that all Lisa has ever done is help him, and there's no way that he couldn't do the same for her. Their mother would turn over in her grave, but she would also flip on her side if they both went to prison. That's why he can't get caught doing everything that he can to help her.

He drops down to search underneath his bed, and that's when he sees it. "Yes!" Crawling underneath the bed, he snatches the credit card and rushes out of his window. He doesn't go out the front door for fear another person may stop him. No one is hardly looking out back, so that's the route he chooses to take. From there he walks at a steady, yet at a fast enough pace with his head down, so that he can make it to a store he's never frequented to make a much needed transaction. The last time he was inside this particular game store was about three years ago, therefore, he's counting on no one knowing his face or name so he can use his credit card with no hitches.

As he walks inside the game store, it's bustling as usual. The place sells every type of gamer equipment and is usually one of the first stores to get new shipments. Lug knows this because he watched each week as the truck came in, but he never had the money to go and splurge on items. Sometimes there's even a line outside of the store of diehard customers ready to get in on the latest technology. He knows what he's here to purchase - the latest game system on the market.

"May I help you, sir?"

"I'm here for the…"

"Let me guess." Without a doubt in his mind, the clerk pulls out the latest game system bundle, complete with controllers and even three games added for a bonus buy of fifty dollars. This is something that Lug can't pass up. He fiddles inside his back pocket for the card.

"Yeah, man, that's it. I ran all the way from work just to get this deal on it."

"That's all everyone has been buying today. Problem is, it's so hot that you have to buy the package deal. The console only versions are no longer available until next week."

"That's cool, man, yeah," Lug says with a flashy smile although his heart races a mile a minute. He pulls out the credit card, but drops it on the floor out of pure nervousness. "Sorry about that, man. You take credit, right?"

"Sure do. Ready to go?"

"Yep," he says, handing the clerk the card. "When I get this home, my kids are gonna love it!" he adds, to throw the clerk off again.

"Oh yeah. This is a beast." As the clerk rings up the order, Lug hopes that nothing gets rejected. He also hopes the clerk doesn't ask for identification, and it's his lucky night. "All clear. Have a good one. Let me put it in a bag for you. Watch your back out here. Don't get robbed."

Lug takes the bag. "Appreciate it." He then walks out and makes a phone call as he walks, holding on tightly to the bag of merchandise. Then, he drops the credit card down into a manhole slit. "Hello? I got something for you if you still want it. Eight hundred flat. They're sold out. Best deal out here. Meet me at ten at the same corner."

Chapter 19

Before leaving the motel, Candyce puts the drugs inside her purse, and covers it with the rest of her items. Lisa goes outside and starts up the car, and they follow behind. Immediately, Lisa puts her sunglasses back on and turns on the engine as soon as both their doors slam shut.

"Let's ride!" Candyce orders as she allows Smack to jump into the back seat. "I'll show you the way."

"Are you gonna drive with those sunglasses on at night?" Jack asks.

"I can see," Lisa responds.

"How?"

"Polarized."

Jack looks over at Candyce who isn't paying him much attention and then back at Lisa who is now pulling out into the intersection. "What is that supposed to mean?"

"Turn right, and then get on the interstate heading two exits down. Get off then." Candyce intercepts.

"Okay," Lisa responds to Candyce, and then she gives Jack his answer. "I can see through them at night anyway. They're made for glare and the sun." Right now, she is using them more as a disguise from the law. She's even forgotten about her black eye.

"What glare? It's nighttime."

"Lights, babe, chill! She might be blinded by the light of this diamond you got for me," she jokes, which results in him reclining in the back seat satisfied with his winning Candyce completely over.

Lisa continues down the road, keeping the radio off and looking out for any signs of road blocks. She knows what she did was pretty well gruesome but regret is nowhere. Robert asked for it, and so did she. The more she thinks about it, the more she wants to scream in rage, but then she accidentally blurts out her emotions.

"Fuck around and cheat…" she mumbles underneath her breath.

"What?" Candyce looks back at Jack, and then back at Lisa who is finding it harder and harder to fight off the anger that only resurfaces when she recalls her dead husband say to his girlfriend *I love you*. Candyce, who thinks the comment is referring to Jack continues, "He better not cheat on me. Fuck you if you do because you won't get this back." She waves the hand in his face that now dons her engagement ring.

"Lisa, you don't even know me like that so how are you gonna start this drama on such a good ass day? We just got engaged," he drags but not offended by the comment made by Lisa at all because he is floating on cloud nine. "For the record," he leans up and pats her on the shoulder, "I know you mean well by what you said. You're just protecting your friend."

"Hell yeah she is! That's my girl. You fuck with us, we kill you. Ain't that right?" Candyce jokes which sends Lisa into a violent cough. "Oh shoot, you alright, girl?" She leans over to grab the steering wheel quickly as Lisa struggles to clear her throat. "Take your foot off the gas and let it roll. Jack, hit her on the back!"

Jack leans up and slugs her two good ones that clear her cough up immediately. Lisa quickly rolls her window down and takes some deep breaths. She then wipes her nose, cheeks and mouth because the tears are all over her face from strangling on her spit which happened to go down the wrong tube when Candyce said what she said.

"I'm okay now," Lisa confirms. "I got it."

Candyce continues to steer as Lisa presses on the gas. "Are you sure? I can't miss this money because you die or we wreck and we all die. The sooner we get this dope off of us the better. No evidence, no arrest." Then, she looks at her ring. "And I can hide this easily just in case they're looking for Jack."

"Thanks you guys, but I can drive now. I just strangled on my own spit," she says quietly.

"Well, here you go. We're almost at the exit." Candyce responds sitting back. "Look, when we get there, I'll get out of the car first and then you Jack. Lisa, you do the same. I have a change of clothes because...I didn't tell you this, Jack, but you're getting sprayed, too."

"What?"

"Yeah, sucks I know, but for the money, spray on. This first stop isn't the place though. I will tell you what car to follow. Everything will be on from there."

That's what Lisa does - every single thing that Candyce says to do. When Candyce says turn right, she turns that way, and when Candyce says turn left, she turns left. When Candyce sees a car pull out from the gas station, she tells Lisa to stay on the road and follow him no matter what.

The drive takes forever as they cut down winding roads that seem to put them back to where they first started. The anonymous car that Lisa follows takes her through one of the toughest neighborhoods there is and then as they exit that neighborhood, she tails him further down the highway until they reach an exit that Lisa has never been down before. Once she gets off, she follows the car through neighborhood to neighborhood for about thirty minutes until they get back on a busy street. At this particular point, Lisa is lost and so is Jack who is looking around curiously in the backseat. The only one at ease is Candyce who knows exactly where she is.

Finally, they drive up to a huge mansion, gated and all, with a flowing fountain in the middle of the yard. As the car pulls inside, a man comes out from by the bushes and shines a light on the license tag which makes Lisa's heart rate rush. She lets out a deep breath and Candyce places her hand atop hers.

"It's cool. Don't start, don't talk and don't act ignorant. Jack, you either."

Someone walks over to the driver's side window at the same time someone else walks over to the passenger's side window. Both Candyce and Lisa get out at the same time, but Candyce rushes to tell Jack to stay seated until they say so.

"Sit down and wait," Candyce says under her breath as she gets out of the car. When she's completely out, she turns to the mountain sized man behind her and speaks. "What's up? Where's Nate?"

"What's up, Candyce. He's inside." He then taps Jack's window, and Jack opens the door to hop out of the backseat. He stares Jack in the face and then turns back to Candyce. Before he speaks, Candyce plugs in a message.

"See!" He flashes her big diamond in the face of security. "I'm engaged now. It just happened. I told you guys this was my man."

"I see," he laughs. "What's up, my man? Congratulations. So you love her, huh?"

"Yeah…" Jack boasts, "And I'll do anything for her."

"Well, regardless, I have to hose you off and her," the man says in reference to Lisa. "Follow me. Candyce, you come, too."

"What? I'm good!" she exclaims.

"Not to be hosed. Just to stay together… and leave the dog."

"Oh." She grips her purse full of drugs and walks behind the two men, Jack, and Lisa all the way to the side of the mansion where there is a guy sitting there with a big hose. When he notices them, he stands up, snaps his fingers, wipes his nose and holds the hose up.

"You can do this with your clothes off or on. It really doesn't matter to me. Don't be ashamed, baby," he addresses Lisa. "I've seen every kind of body there is, and yours isn't an exception, sweetheart."

Lisa glances at Candyce, and Candyce mouths the word *sorry* back her way. As Lisa turns back to look the hose man in the face, she starts to take off her shoes, but then thinks about already having been wet from head to toe earlier today. It didn't kill her, so she slides her foot back inside her shoe and nods to the expectant hose man to go ahead and spray. Jack starts to take off his clothes. As soon as Jack tosses his last garment to the side, the hose man fires away – not at Jack but at Lisa.

Water hits her directly on her chest and then she catches it in the legs and back. The whole thing takes less than fifteen seconds, but by the end, Lisa is boiling over with rage as she watches Jack stand there naked the whole time with only a drop or two of water on him resulting from the splash. When the hose man turns the water off, he tosses Lisa a towel.

"Put your damn clothes back on, man," he says to Jack. Then he looks at Lisa. "It makes more sense to take your clothes off so we can see if we need to kill your ass. At least you won't get wet."

"You're not gonna hose him? Seriously?" Lisa asks as her chopped up blunt haircut quickly retracts into a multitude of ripples and waves.

"Seriously," he answers. "Candyce, pat her down."

"What!" she looks at Candyce in horror.

"I have to, sis. At least it's me though, right?"

"Or do you want me to finish up? Your call, little lady," he asks as Candyce pats her down. "You look better curly. I'm not playing. It's nice. No harm done," he says as he glares at Candyce. "It's your hand to the gun and also catching a bullet." Then he walks back to his seat.

Lisa begins to ring out her shirt, totally pissed off at Candyce for not telling her about the undress and stay dressed part of the whole game. "Just what the hell does he mean…hand to the gun and catch the bullet? You're wrong for this, girl. Dead wrong."

"Well, that's what he means, Lisa. Dead. It'll be my fault if they shoot you because I'm the one who gave you the clear by patting you down, and then I'll catch a bullet in the head for deliberately setting them up. Good thing we're all good though because Nate doesn't play!" she laughs. "Your shoes are squeaking. Take 'em off. Wear mine. You know we're just about the same size."

"We don't wear the same size in shoes! Can't you just drop the drugs and have someone bring you the money? Why all this formality?"

"No, chill. You're worse than Jack. Did you see him back there?" she whispers as she grins at Jack who tags along behind, unable to hear what Candyce is saying because the other guard is keeping him separate from the ladies.

"Of course I saw him. That's not funny, Candyce. Come on! That's your fiancé," Lisa responds to her careless and carefree best friend.

"I know," she winks with a smirk. "He sure is mine...all mine," she sings as we turn the corner into a huge room with two cascading, crystal chandeliers placed directly in the middle of the vaulted ceilings. The floor beneath their feet was spotless and obviously polished because as soon as Lisa steps onto it she has to balance herself with her arms to keep from plummeting.

"Oh shoot, Lisa, watch out!" Before Candyce could grab her, one of the so-called guards snatches her by her arm.

"Put on these." He hands her some cotton footies to roll onto her shoes.

"You could've given me these before I even got on this damn floor," Lisa snatches them away from his hand annoyed and feeling like she has absolutely nothing to lose, until he quickly reminds her.

"I could have done a lot more things back there, namely one, but you're still standing."

Lisa takes the threat seriously and slides on the thick cotton socks. Then, she viciously cuts her eyes at Candyce who has no idea about the amount of stress she's under as she waits for this illegal payday to put some money in her pocket. Candyce simply looks back her way and says, "It's almost over. Sorry. You won't regret it just this one time. Seriously."

Lisa rolls her eyes in hopes that absolutely none of the people who have seen her so far recognize her from some flash photo of herself on the news. She knows that her name is already out there, so she's hoping for a smooth transaction when it comes to Candyce and that no one asks too many questions. As Lisa regains her wet composure, she starts to shiver as a man walks out into the open from another room.

His gait is really fast, as if he's in the biggest rush of his life. When he comes closer to a flawless white couch, he dives onto it and pulls out a small rectangular box that he as underneath it. Then, he opens it to reveal a load of cash. When he looks up, he claps his hands and puts a big smile on his face as he waves us forward. We start walking, but he stops us with the palm of his hand.

"No, no. Just Candyce. You got it, baby?"

"Baby?" Jack retorts.

The guy looks at Jack for a second or two and afterwards, places his attention back on the lady with the goods. Then, he gives Lisa some attention as well.

"What's up, Lisa," the guy surprisingly says.

Lisa appears confused, but then speaks back. "Hi."

"Lisa, this is Nate," Candyce introduces them. "Nate, this is Lisa as you already know and Jack."

"Her fiancé!" Jack shouts resulting in a guard smacking him in the back of his head. "Ouch, man chill." Jack then looks over at Lisa. "Lisa, you know him?"

"Now I do. That's Nate." He's a funny looking young man. His hair is cut with a military groove to it, and his clothing is really loose on him, like silk falls on a very skinny man. Nate stares Candyce up and down as she walks over to him, and when she sits down, he immediately reaches for her left hand and ring finger. Candyce happily shows it to him, and while her hand is inside his, he whispers something in her ear. She nods and takes her hand away. Then, she looks up at Jack and Lisa before removing the drugs from her purse.

Another man from the back comes out, but doesn't say one word. Instead of speaking, when he gets close enough to the drugs, he picks the packages up, takes a scale from underneath the center table, weighs it and then he sniffs it. About ten seconds go by as he stands there before walking back out of the room.

"Good deal!" Nate's hands clap together loudly as he then waves Lisa and Jack over. Hesitantly, they both come, Lisa in her socks and Jack wrapped up inside his fury over Nate's handling of Candyce's hand and ring finger.

Jack whispers to Lisa, "I should suffocate his ass in those drugs."

"But you won't though."

"What makes you think I won't?"

"Because of the men with the guns." Lisa looks around. At each corner of the room, there is someone holding a weapon. "Let's not make a scene before we become a permanent part of the scene."

Lisa takes a seat in an empty couch on the side closer to Candyce purposely so that Jack has more than arm space between himself and Nate. Jack is very impulsive. Therefore, it would be more than reckless to allow them to be too close to one another.

"It's nice to meet you, Jack. Man to man, Candyce is a gem. Know what I mean? She's always had my back, and I've always had hers. Trust her like she's my own arm, so from me to you, blessings."

"Blessings?"

"Sure. It's not like you're going to meet her parents anytime soon, so I'd like to give you my blessing to marry her."

Candyce's mouth remains sealed shut as she stares back at Jack intently. Jack pays her no attention.

"Fuck a blessing. She said yes, so it's on. As far as her parents, I'll meet them soon enough. They can bless me then. Are you two done?"

There is complete silence in the room. Lisa's hand slowly reaches up to her black eye, but that's when Nate intervenes. "Get the lady a cold pack. Is Jack always this sensitive? Aren't blessings a good thing, Lisa?"

"Yes…and thanks, but it's okay. Just a little sore. I can tolerate it."

"Tolerate it?" Nate laughs. "Tolerate pain? Torture sucks. It looks like you've been through enough already. Get the lady some dry clothes, too," he orders his men. Then he looks at Jack with a smirk. "The clothes in my lady's room should fit her just fine."

Jack peers over at Candyce who is busy scratching her leg without a care in the world, and then he scolds Nate with his eyes. Thankfully, Jack keeps his mouth shut, sits back and waits to leave. A man with the cold pack comes in for Lisa, and on the far end of the room a man brings another package toward Nate.

"Here's an extra ten." Nate grabs the package and then hands it to Candyce who looks at the money uncomfortably. "Buy yourself a wedding dress."

"Let's go, Candyce!" Jack commands angrily, and a guard comes up behind him with his gun ready. Nate backs him away, however, with a flick of his hand.

"A hot head!" he pauses. "I'm gonna clue you in, Jack. She likes her men to take it easy. Relax a little bit." He turns back to Candyce with a stone face. "You did good. Get outta here, babe."

"Thanks, Nate. Come on, guys. Let's go. Smack's a-waiting!" Candyce stuffs all the money in her purse and stands there waiting on her friends to get up. When Jack elevates from his seat, he storms by Candyce angrier than ever. Candyce ignores the show, and Lisa simply gets up without the change of clothes.

"They'll have your clothes at the door, sweetheart."

"Oh…" She turns to look back at him. "Thanks again."

He nods and watches as they walk out, escorted by the same men that took them inside. What Nate said would happen, happened; her clothes are at the door waiting on her. Lisa turns them down, however, deciding that it isn't such a great idea to take clothing from someone who may need a favor down the road.

Chapter 20

Head down and eyes up, Lug stands at the corner of Bush and Knotts Roads waiting on his connect, the one that's been dying for the latest game system. The neighborhood, which is many blocks from the game store, isn't that safe, but in this area, lots of people know him and vice versa. Therefore, just this fact alone makes him feel slightly safer than if he stands elsewhere in unknown territory.

He watches diligently as cars pass by, holding on tightly to his bag of merchandise in hopes that his buyer comes quickly. His gut wants to bottom out each time a person walks his way on the sidewalk. Even though he's extremely paranoid that someone will take his only way of getting this money right out of the palm of his hand, no one does. The buyer finally pulls up.

"Hey, man, get in."

Without thinking about anything, Lug hops inside the car. "Thanks, man. I just got it, and it's fully loaded. Check it out." Lug opens the huge bag and pulls out the game system with three games to match. The buyer locks the doors of the car as he checks out the merchandise inside Lug's lap. "You got the money? Eight hundred, man. I gotta get going. Give it to you for seven hundred flat."

"Yeah, hold up. Lemme get it." The buyer reaches inside his pocket, fiddles around a little bit and then pulls out the money, prepared to count it out to Lug. "Twenties good, man? That's all I got."

"Yeah, lemme have it." Lug holds out his hand as the man counts the money up inside his palm.

"My kids have been waiting on this and so have I. Thanks, man. That's forty, sixty, and then we got one hundred, two hundred. Three…"

"Wait a minute. Time out. Back that up," Lug requests firmly as he inspects the money that lands into his hand. "You got fives mixed in here, man!"

The buyer removes his money from Lug's hand and shifts through it. "Oh, man, my bad. I had the money all mixed up at home, but I got the twenties…hold up."

Lug gets uneasy and grabs his bag of merchandise, reaches for the door handle, but it's locked. When he goes to open it, he feels a piece of metal at the back of his neck. The windows of the car are tinted to the max, and in the dark, it's nearly impossible to see inside unless a passer-by is standing right up on the vehicle. Therefore, Lug knows he's caught with nowhere to go.

He drops the bag on the floor board of the car and raises his hands in the air. "Man, look, I just want my money. That's all. If you don't have it, that's all you had to say. It's only right that I take my stuff and move on."

"It's only right that I take your stuff and move on, Lug." The man pokes the piece of metal harder behind Lug's ear. "I heard your sister's name on television today. That's some sick shit. Both of you think you can just get over…should turn her ass in. Get more money plus this game system. You know where she's at?"

"Reward? My sister is just going in for questioning. That's it! I don't know where she is. Your fucking guess is as good as mine!" Lug hits the window, and the guy with the gun goes crazy.

"Don't hit my shit!" He slams Lug's head against the same window Lug just hit, and then shouts again. "Don't hit my shit! Where is she? When they offer a reward for her ass, I'm getting it."

Lug gets infuriated each time he thinks about not only getting robbed for his goods, but also, each time the guy talks about turning in his sister, Lisa. Being succumb by his rage, Lug shoves back against the arm of his attacker, pinning his arm between the seat and begins to pound him in his throat and face. Continuing to press his full body weight against the assailant's arm, he continues to pound him as hard as he can, believing that he's fighting for his life. Lug backs off as he watches the guy's head fall forward onto the gear shift, blood leaking everywhere from his face. He reaches to feel for a pulse at the man's throat and wrist, and what he feels is very light.

"Oh hell no," he cries. That's when he sees it. On the floor board of the backseat, there's a gun, but it's not real. Lug picks it up and notices he's seen this before in an antique toy store a long time ago. "A sticker...What the fu...?" Tears begin to roll from his eyes as he turns the gun around. "A toy?" he asks quietly as his palms shake. He throws the toy gun down so hard again against the floor that it comes apart, grabs his bag and before jumping from the car, he sits the assaulted guy up in the seat, turns the music up and exits. "No problem, man. No problem, homey! Good seeing you. Take it easy. He should be here in about fifteen minutes. Just stay put," he says out loud, just in case someone is watching and listening.

After he slams the door, he walks down the street, visibly shaken by the event that just took place. Maintaining his cool the best he knows how, he crosses the street to get to an open area to try and call his sister once

136

more. The park is right up the road, and he plans on disappearing in a party going crowd.

His feet pound the pavement, and although he is deathly afraid to look back at the car he just fled, he does anyway. His eyes meet with two men pointing his way. One of the men starts to dial on the phone as he tries to open the driver's side door and the other is running Lug's way. There's no time to think. Lug takes off running, merchandise and all.

"Oh God, oh God, help me please. Don't let him die," he mumbles as he runs as fast as he can. Instead of heading to the park, he turns the corner quickly trying to lose his tailer. There's an alley way between two houses, so he decides to cut through it. That's a big mistake because there's a line of bushes covering the exit, so he turns around only to come face to face with the person that follows behind. "Look, man, I swear I didn't do nothing!"

"Hell you mean, you didn't do nothing? My man's back there leaning on the window looking bad as fuck, and you mean you didn't do something? Gimme that shit out your hand!"

Lug looks down at his bag. "Is this what this is about?"

"Hell yeah, it's what it's about! We were waiting on that shit."

"You were there?" Lug asks stalling for time. He glances up at some people who are now peeping through their blinds at the noise in between their homes. This is exactly what Lug wants. "Look, man, don't rob me for my goods!" he yells, thinking that someone in one of the homes will rush to help or call the police. Just then, the other man comes around the corner, and this one has a pistol in his right hand aiming it directly at Lug's chest. Lug throws the bag of merchandise directly at the man with the gun and turns to run toward the bushes when the gun goes off. Lug falls to the ground, feeling the rush of pain from a bullet hitting him in the back.

Moans only exacerbate the agony he feels as he crawls along the ground, looking up at the windows for help, but the people in the windows close the blinds. He hears footsteps behind him, but they quickly begin to retreat; the men telling each other to head back to the car. That's when he pulls out his cell phone to dial. The phone rings and rings, but he gets no answer.

Chapter 21

"I'm gonna climb back here with Jack while you drive, Lisa, so we can count out this money. I know you're quite pissed, so let me just…" she says not completing her statement as she slides back into the arms of Jack who finishes pulling her back onto the back seat. Then as she moves Smack to the front with Lisa, she looks over at him. "We just came off big in cash, and I'm still your lady, remember? Don't be mad at me, babe. Nate is good people." She leans over and kisses him on his cheek and then tells Lisa to just hit the highway. "Here, Jack. Count this stack."

"You always make me look like a joke, babe. Always. You let that dude disrespect me…"

"Well," she sighs, looking back up at Lisa. "Hit the highway, Lisa," she commands in a more authoritative tone.

"I already heard you, Candyce," she responds as she continues to look at her phone as it shows Lug's number continuously. He's dialing over and over again, and it's starting to make Lisa nervous. "Don't tell me to hit the highway again."

"Just hurry up. We need to get off this street about now."

"Is that what this is, Candyce? You ignore me now for some money?" Jack asks.

Lisa finally veers off onto the highway as Jack continues to complain about being ignored, and that's when she hears a gunshot, causing her to swerve but maintain control of the car. "What the fuck was that, Candyce! Oh shit! You just shot him!" Jack's head hits the back of her Uncle Joe's car seat, and then he slumps over onto the window. His head leans forward while his eyes stare into the driver's side mirror between his door and the driver's seat. "Get his ass up from looking at me! Candyce, what the hell?"

As Lisa goes down the ramp that leads to the merge into traffic, Candyce opens the door and kicks Jack down into a large ditch that follows the ramp downward. A dead Jack rolls slowly down the hill into the thick bushes and Candyce shuts the door, adjusts her ring, and places the pistol back inside her purse.

"What the hell was that?" Lisa frantically asks again.

Candyce climbs into the front seat, nearly hyperventilating from what she just did. Then, she immediately puts stacks of money directly into Lisa's lap. "I told you I would hook you up. He was just my flunky." She picks up Smack once again and places her into the back seat. "Go on now, baby. It's alright."

"What? You just shot the man in the head who just gave you that expensive ass ring out of one of the top jewelry stores in the damn state! On top of that, he professed his undying love for you and even helped you traffic some damn dope!"

"No shit, Lisa! I didn't ask him to do any dumb shit like the first two things you said either. What was I suppose to do? Would you turn this big ass ring down over principle?" She looks back behind the car and still there's no traffic. "I love this part of town. People have so much money until they don't see a damn thing!" She stares at Lisa, thinking of something to say to get her to understand.

"Girl, he had to die. Nate doesn't play keeping flunkies alive." She looks down at her bag, thinking that the gun may be making Lisa more nervous that what she needs to be. "The gun is actually his piece. They'll be coming to get it from me in about a week, so don't think I own a gun because I don't. I prefer not to either…even though my dad taught me how to use one…" she stammers until Lisa interrupts.

"Is this what you do? Am I a flunky, too? Are you about to blast my head off, C, huh?" Lisa is so afraid that she literally shakes the steering wheel unsteady, causing Candyce to reach over and steer.

"Girl, I wouldn't kill you! You're my girl. I just gave you practically half the money. Just like I said I would hook you up, I did! Just drive. Nate is gonna clean that up. That's dumping ground far enough away from his house and close enough for them to get the flunkies out without being seen. Your phone is ringing. It's been ringing constantly."

Lisa just stares blankly at the road, but finally picks up. "Lug, listen to me. I had your stuff, but I already dumped it. It's gone, okay," she lies. "Lug? Lug!" She hears him breathing but he's not answering fast enough. Finally, she hears his voice.

"Lisa, Lisa, sis…I tried to get some money…"

"Lug, I know that. I took the bag, and you won't get it back. Get back to work, Lug. That's what's important right now." He doesn't answer. "Lug?"

"They shot me, sis."

She tunes in to his rapid breathing on the telephone, and panics, "Lug, where are you, baby boy? Why are you breathing like that? Lug!" she screams through the phone.

"I'm near the park, sis," he sighs. "I tried...I'm in between the houses across from the park...I love you, Lisa. I need some help, sis. They shot me in the back."

"Lug! Lug!" Lisa holds the phone in the air as she floors it down the highway, not caring about anything or anyone at the moment but her baby brother.

"Lisa, what is it? What's wrong?"

"It's Lug! Something's wrong with Lug! He's been shot, C!"

"What!" Candyce screams. "Shot!" She looks back down the road where she dumped Jack's body then back at the road ahead, fastening her seatbelt. "Where is he? Shot like shot?"

"He's on the phone right now, but he's dying! Call the cops!"

"Hell no, I can't call 911 from this phone, Lisa. They'll trace us, and we have all this cash on us! I just dumped a body!"

"Lug!" she hollers, but still no answer. "We have to go to the park. That's where he is. Lug, don't die, baby! Breathe!" She hears him breathing on the phone. "Dammit!" She slams her hands against the steering wheel. "Lug, I'm coming! I'm on my way. I'm coming to the park. I need you to hang up and call 911 now. Do it now!"

"Okay," he answers faintly. "I love you." The phone hangs up.

"God!" Lisa cries, looking up to the sky. "Not my brother, please! I'm sorry! I'm so sorry!"

"Look, Lisa, just drive. Drive as fast as you can without getting us pulled over. Lug needs us, and we can't have any cops on our tail. Not now anyway. There's just too much going on, and…"

Candyce continues to talk and as she's talking, Lisa slants her eyes over at whom she thought was her best friend. Lisa's whole outlook about Candyce changes as she drives as fast as she can to where she can help her dying brother, but at the same time, she wonders if she's going to make it away from Candyce alive at all.

From her periphery, Candyce's purse sits open on the floor board with both the pistol and the money in plain view. She's not so adamant about counting the cash anymore. Then, she takes a look at the cash Candyce sat in her lap and starts to truly believe that her fate will be like the flunky Jack's.

"You hear me, girl. Everything is going to be just fine. Relax your mind and drive. Don't get into a daze on me now, or you can pull over so I can drive. You hear me?"

Lisa snaps out of her paranoia for a second to answer, "Yeah, I understand. I got it. He's gonna be fine," she says over and over under her breath. "My baby brother is gonna be fine." She wipes the tears that drain from the corners of her eyes nonstop. Feeling tempted to call his phone again, she continues to look at it but doesn't, afraid that she'll interrupt the signal from his phone to emergency dispatch. "Candyce, I need the quickest way to the park."

"Just keep going. It's the park down the road from his apartment complex right?"

"Yeah, that's the only one he goes to. That's it. It wouldn't be another park. Everytime he says the damn word park, that's the park he's talking about."

"Calm down and drive, Lisa. It's a straight shot. Actually, we can cut through…"

"Wait, I know how to get there even faster."

Lisa jerks the car off onto the next exit and then her phone rings again. It's her Aunt Lyndi, and she swiftly answers, "Hello, Ma! Ma!"

"Lisa, where are you?"

"Ma, I need you to go to the park by Lug's place. Hurry up, Ma, please. Get in the car now! Lug's been shot. He's shot, Ma!"

"Oh Jesus, please, not my baby boy," Lyndi screams, and the phone drops. As soon as it drops, Lisa hears her Uncle Joe snatch it up and start speaking.

"Hello, Lisa. What…"

"I don't have time, Uncle Joe! Lug is dying in between some homes across the street from the park. Please go out there now. He told me he was shot in the back. Don't call him, just go! He's out there alone dying, Uncle Joe. I'm on my way out there. Please!"

That's the end of the conversation. Lisa pulls the phone away from her ear, looks at the connection, and the timer is flashing. Candyce then takes her phone.

"Let me hold it, hon. I'll keep it on me and make sure to answer any and all calls coming in while you just get there. I'm right here with you. Right here with you," she continues, glancing out the rear view mirror to make sure no authorities are coming behind them.

"I can hold on to my own phone, Candyce," Lisa quickly states, combating her friend's awkward generosity. She holds her hand out, but Candyce insists.

"I got it. Just drive. The quicker we get there, the better."

Lisa glances over at Candyce who still doesn't know that the cops are hunting her for murder. The hunt is still on, and now, they are probably more on her trail than they have been all day. As she drives, she stares at the road in a total fog until she turns off the current street and onto a busier street causing Candyce's bag to fall to the side. As Candyce picks it up and stuffs all the money back inside the bag, Lisa's mind races and her paranoia kicks in.

"So how did Nate have clothes for me? Like, how did he know what size I am and all?"

"What?" Candyce asks, placing her feet around her bag and fiddling with her fingernails. Lisa only watches her best friend, beginning to imagine her as someone other than the girl she thought she knew.

"I mean, he had clothes ready to fit me already at his big ass house, and I heard how he said that to Jack, almost to make him mad."

Candyce turns to look at Lisa in disbelief, and then she suddenly throws her head back in laughter, slamming it against the head rest. "Okay! Oh my gosh, you're good!" she confesses. "I figured you would guess but not that quickly! Nate, well, he's kind of my boyfriend. He's been my boyfriend for a while now, so that's kinda why he had clothes to fit you."

"So Jack…" Lisa interjects.

"No, like I said, he was a flunky."

"What's so funny?"

"Look, Lisa," she continues, wiping the grin from her face. "You know who I am. You're my sister, and if you think that I'm setting you up as well, you're dead wrong. I just need to put this money up and find out why those cops were at my house. If it was because of Jack, well, he's dead, and they'll never find him. If it's because of the drugs, well, I never keep them at home. They're always with Nate, and you're my girl so you won't tell, right?"

Lisa doesn't answer until she takes a deep breath. "You should have told me."

"Well, now you know. Nothing's changed." To confirm her loyalty she adds, "I haven't shot you at all. I had to get rid of him…Nate ordered me, too. I gave you the money and all that."

"I'm driving," Lisa comments. "You can't shoot the driver, now can you? Especially when you're in the passenger's seat," she grins and looks over at her friend who is turning a candy apple complexion. Lisa notices her color, but continues talking though not trusting. "And nothing will change between us, Candyce. Nothing will. I love you, girl."

"Love you, too, Lisa. Thanks, and I'm really sorry for everything. I had to kill him. I had to or it's my own throat." Candyce continues in pleas for sympathy. Lisa listens and continues to drive, constantly eyeing the bag on the floor that contains the pistol, cash and her cell phone. Lisa drives in silence until she comes within one block of the park. That's when her attention goes off of Candyce and onto the onslaught of cops in the area. She continues to drive slowly forward until she finds the perfect place to park and watch.

Lisa's tears begin to break through her eyes as she puts on the car's brake. A crowd of people are standing across the street on the curb while the cops form a barrier on the sidewalk. That's when Lisa spots her aunt and uncle on the scene, and in a knee jerk response, opens her driver's side door. As soon as she opens it, she shuts it back.

"Go on! Go! That's your brother!" Candyce yells. "I'll be right here waiting. I can't get out with you because I don't know what the cops were doing at my house, but you can go. Lisa," she continues to yell. "Get out of the car!"

"I can't!" Her eyes swell at Candyce, and then she screams again, squeezing her head in between her hands while the veins in her neck ripple under her skin. "I can't dammit! Oh God, oh God, help me!"

Candyce reaches over to touch her, but when she does, Lisa swings her arm to knock her away, accidentally scratching the side of Candyce's face. "Ouch! Lisa, cut that shit out! You just scratched me on the side of my face." She leans over, pulls down the visor and inspects her face in the mirror by pulling on her cheek. The scratch didn't break her skin, however, there's a long, red mark running from her nose to the base of her ear. "Damn! What did you do that for?"

"They're looking for me!"

Candyce flips her hair out of her face and turns to face Lisa, one of her hands on the dash board and one on the seat. Her face flushes red again and her breathing goes rapid. Lisa doesn't even turn her way because at this point, she doesn't care about anything but her brother. If he's dead, then she's dead.

"What do you mean they? Who is they?" Candyce asks as she looks out the window where all the cops are circling and controlling the crowd. Then, she rolls her eyes and nervously taps on the dash with her fingers until Lisa burst into tears again. This doesn't phase Candyce though. It only makes her more anxious about the situation she's in being that she has drug money still on her and just shoved an ex she shot out by the highway. She hauls herself over into Lisa's driver's side space, grabs her by the face and stares her in her weeping eyes. "You tell me who is looking for you!"

"I killed him," Lisa cries softly as her face quivers in the hands of Candyce.

"Fuck!" Candyce drops her hands, looks over at the cops again and then back at Lisa. "Who the fuck did you kill, Lisa? Answer me!" No matter how much Candyce stares and screams, Lisa doesn't say a word. The only things making any kind of sense to Candyce right now are the tears. As she looks back toward the area between the homes where an ambulance is stalled, she sees a stretcher. Then, she lightly pushes her sobbing friend's face to the horrible scene.

"No! No, God! No, Jesus, no!" Lisa collapses into the arms of her friend who doesn't know what to do for her anymore. There are people everywhere, and it isn't safe for her to get out of the car because she isn't sure what Lisa is talking about when she said she killed him.

As Lisa cries and screams non-stop, passers-by are becoming aware of her commotion although it's nightfall. Therefore, Candyce turns on the radio as high as she can turn it to block out the sound. As the radio plays, she slumps over and begins to weep with her friend who is continuously crying over what could be her now deceased younger brother.

"Wait, wait, listen!" Candyce tries to silence Lisa as she moans, but her pleas for Lisa to quiet down don't work. The radio announcer starts to talk about the incident, a shooting, at the park. "She's talking about your brother Lug."

Lisa sits up, visibly shaken as she focuses in on what the radio announcer is saying. Her eyes shift to the ambulance and all the people around, but then she hears her brother's name.

"A name has been released of the man who is shot – Luscious Caldwell - and I wonder if it's in any way connected to what was on the news earlier today about a Lisa Caldwell who reportedly might have killed some people inside her house. By listening to all the information, these crimes could be related if we look at the last names. As it's unraveling on the news, Sandra," the radio personality continues, "it seems like this could be a domestic dispute gone down the wrong path because there are two people dead on Lincoln street and now this shooting with the same name attached, maybe even a sibling rivalry... Sandra, they say this Lisa Caldwell is married, so could this Luscious Caldwell that just got shot be her husband's brother? I'm no detective, but something's fishy. Call in and let us know what you think..."

Lisa shoves away from Candyce and turns the radio off. Then, she sits up straight in the car, staring ahead as she shoves her sunglasses on. She puts the gear in drive, but before she takes off, Candyce stops her by grabbing her arm and throwing it off the steering wheel.

"Lisa Caldwell? Lisa, that's you," she states, consumed by confusion. "What fuckin' murders, Lisa?"

"Nothing!"

"Like hell it's nothing! That's you they're talking about, Lisa Caldwell," she says stressing the last name. "You never took Robert's last name remember! Lug is your fuckin' brother, not his." Candyce states as her phone starts to ring. When she looks down at it, she sees that it's Nate. "Dammit!" She ignores it and stares back at Lisa waiting for an answer about what she just heard on the radio. "Is this the shit you've been acting all weird about? Did you kill somebody, Lisa? Are you the reason why the cops were at my house? Where's my damn car?" she screams, and Lisa just sits in the seat with the car running watching her Uncle Joe and Ma run back to their other car.

When she watches them get inside the car, she proceeds to follow closely behind them until she finds out what hospital Lug is going to be held in. Her hand is itching to call on the phone, but she doesn't believe that she can bear any horrible news about her only sibling on earth being dead. She rushes around another block to meet her aunt and uncle head on at an intersecting road to avoid the plethora of cops, and as Candyce is still yelling at the top of her lungs at her, she ends up at a traffic light. To the left are her Uncle Joe and Aunt Lyndi, and when they recognize Lisa sitting their car, they stare hopelessly while Lisa does likewise.

"Who is that? Lisa, who the hell is that?" Candyce asks, bouncing up and down in the chair and hitting the dash while she covers her face with her hair. Lisa's phone rings. Immediately, she puts the car in park, reaches over a hyper Candyce, and dumps her entire bag of money on the floor board until her phone becomes visible. Then, she answers without saying a word, but her Aunt Lyndi can see her face with the help of the street lights.

"Baby, he's alive! Barely, but he's alive. We're going up the street, at the same hospital where y'all were born," she cries.

Lisa drops the phone and begins to sob, and the traffic light changes. She watches as her Uncle Joe stares back at her stone faced as he crosses the intersection. Candyce then taps Lisa, breaking her from her trance so that she can turn right to follow behind them. Candyce's phone rings again. She looks up at Lisa who is staring ahead at the road, and then she looks back at her phone. She picks it up and begins to talk as Lisa spins the wheel slowly to the right, staying a good distance behind her relatives.

"Yeah, yeah, I have it, and I took care of that already. I'm not home though," Candyce answers whoever it is she's talking to on the telephone. "Uhm hmm, yeah." Then after a brief and awkward silence, she puts the phone face down on the seat in between her legs. Then she stares over at her friend Lisa and asks nothing but loaded questions. "What's going on, Lisa? Be straight with me. Why are you on the news? The cops must be looking for you because you killed Robert, huh, and who else? You've been on a damn killing spree while I was away and didn't say shit?"

Lisa doesn't answer the question aloud. She only continues to drive as Candyce's question triggers her thoughts back to when she was on her way home to try and make up with Robert. As she was thinking of all kinds of ways to make his life better with her, she never thought for one second that he'd already started making someone else's life better while ripping hers apart. She remembers calling him from the car on her way back home, but he didn't answer. That was probably when they were eating the dinner she cooked for him or either ripping each other's clothes off as they groped each other down the hallway. They could have even been in the process of making love, the way Lisa thought he should have been making love to her.

"Lisa...Lisa? You hear me?" Candyce asks, slowly leaning over to reach into her bag. This movement catches Lisa's eye, and she answers quickly and in a fit of rage.

"Yeah, I heard you," she states through the grind of her teeth as she spins the car into a barren parking lot, driving all the way to the back of the lot away from the street. Candyce's head bangs against the window as a result of the hard unexpected turn, but she notices that her head doesn't stop banging. The ashtray from the car is gripped inside of Lisa's hand and she plummets the side of Candyce's head over and over again with all the strength of her right hand.

"Stop! Help me!" Candyce screams as she scrambles to fight back, but Lisa's already pulled the brake on the car and is now using both hands to hurl more blows to the side of her skull. Candyce's hand reaches for the lock, but each time she tries to pull it, the strikes against her head result in her losing her grip and falling defenseless.

"Hello? Hello, Candyce?" a voice on the face down cell phone hollers through the speaker, causing Lisa to glance down where it fell during the attack. She looks around the area in the barren parking lot, and then she picks up the phone to a familiar voice continuing to call Candyce. Instead of saying anything, Lisa leans the friend she just attacked back in the seat. Then, she leans the seat back as well, draping Candyce's blonde hair over her face so that she looks like she's fast asleep. Lisa's ears still pick up the sound of the voice calling for Candyce as she sits back into the driver's seat.

Lisa taps her lap and Smack jumps into the front seat with her as she holds the phone up to her ear. Smack's tongue is wagging and she's panting heavily into the speaker of the phone. Then she jumps over on top of her owner and begins to lick her wounds. Lisa takes one last listen to the voice she knows as Nate, and then she finally answers him.

"Fuck you. She's dead. Now you can come pick her ass up if you can find her," she cries as she glances over at her dead friend. Then, she vomits all over the floor board beneath her feet. When she gets the air to speak again, she continues, sobbing bitterly, "I know you told her to kill me. If you send the cops for me, then I'll send them for you." Then, she hangs up the phone. "I'm sorry, Candyce. Just like you had to, I had to." Lisa shoves the money back inside the bag and drives on to the hospital.

Chapter 22

"Oh, Joe, I can't do this. I can't do this anymore. I can't!"

"Listen, Lyndi!" he commands sternly, grabbing her at the shoulders as they get ready to exit the car in the emergency room parking lot. "Just listen! We have got say something now! We've got to! Do you want to go to prison? Lug is in there shot and possibly dead. The cops are everywhere, and if they put two and two together, we are bound to get questioned. She's in my car, Lyndi."

"I know that! I know!" she screams angrily. "But that's our niece, and that's our nephew in there fighting for his life. They're both fighting for their lives, Joe, and I'm not helping no cop or anybody until I know every single fact of what's going on. Do you understand that? I don't throw my family to the dogs!" She opens her car door, but turns back to her husband who is at a loss of words on what to do next when they enter the hospital. "As far as I'm concerned, we hadn't been at home, and she took the car without us knowing." Then, she gets out and slams the door.

"You said she changed clothes in the house, Lyndi!" he yells, but goes silent when he exits the car, pretending to walk with his wife like Lug is the only person they are praying for at the moment. His eyes can't help but shift the same as Lyndi's because they are well aware that Lisa is following them and isn't far behind.

The sliding doors come open and Lyndi rushes to the emergency room sign in to get clearance to see Lug. Joe stands beside her rubbing the top of his head and looking around when his eyes catch the television. Nothing is playing about the shooting nor the murders reported at Lisa's house, and when he hears Lyndi slap the counter in front of them and scream at the administrator, he snaps out of his paranoia.

"Lyndi!" he exclaims, grabbing her wrists as she struggles to pull away. The security guard looks over at them, and he quickly leans in to her ear and whispers, "You have got to calm down or security will put us out of here. Now calm down." He then turns to the administrator at the counter and apologizes, "We just watched our nephew come in here, we were on the scene where he was shot, and we really need to see him. We're his only family. His mom is dead, and this has been his mom since then, although she's really his aunt, so please…how can we…"

"Sir, sir, we can put you in a room back in the back I'm sure, but let me get things situated and have someone talk to the doctor so we can see where things are headed. Please, wait here, and I'll open the door for you as I can see she's severely distraught. I understand. When I press the button, come on back," the administrator allows.

As Joe allows Lyndi to lean on him, he turns to look out of the hospital's long glass windows and behind the parked cars on the street is Lisa staring back at him. When their eyes meet, he stops, taps Lyndi and directs her eyes that way. Just as fast as he does that, he swiftly turns her away into the opened doorway leading to a private room where they can sit and wait. Before they get to the room, Lyndi's phone vibrates on her leg.

"Hello?" she answers it.

"Thank you, ma'am. Thank you so much," Joe states as the nurse closes the door behind her. He sits Lyndi down on a chair while he sits beside her, rubbing his hands together briskly to try and calm his nerves while praying to the Lord under his breath.

"Lisa, Lisa, baby, what's going on?" she cries, but Joe comes over to calm her down so that she can speak quieter.

"These walls have ears, Lyndi," he says rubbing her shoulders. Although Lyndi starts the questioning of her niece, she can't continue because all that comes from her mouth are moans and wails so bad that any person walking by the door would think that she's in bodily distress. Just as Joe is about to take the phone, there's a knock at the door. "Press mute," he says to Lyndi, but she doesn't listen. Instead, she sits the phone down on the chair, and the door comes open.

**

"Hello? Hello, Ma?" I shout into the phone about to lose all cool until I hear Uncle Joe say the words press mute, so that's what I do. In the background, I hear different voices so I press my head against the phone to hear what they're going to say about Lug. Someone then beeps their car horn at me, forcing me to move over into a parking space. This is the one thing that I don't want to do because it traps me in. After pulling inside the park, I concentrate on the conversation going on inside the hospital room.

"Hello, and I'm sorry to have to come to you at such a critical time, but I have good news. I'm Dr. Randall Lewis, and I hear that you're the only family of the patient. He also has you on his records. He's a healthy young man, but as you know, he's been shot in the back. The bullet went straight through him, missing every single major organ that could have killed him. That being said, he's going to be alright. I'm a believer in Jesus' goodness just as Luscious told me you are, so keep praying that He be with us in the room as we work to get your son back in good shape. The bullet exited through his chest up near his right shoulder, missing his heart and all. He's in much pain, but we have him sedated so that we can monitor him, fix him back up, keep him for some nights and things of that nature. It looks like he will make it, so you don't have too much to worry about now. He's going to pull through, I'm ninety percent confident."

Ma starts to shout and praise God while I listen to Uncle Joe thank the doctor for looking after Lug. My heart goes from heavy to extremely thankful to God, but as soon as I thank the only One Who can forgive me for all my sins, I look over at a dead Candyce who lay there with Smack on her lap. I'm overwhelmed with an emotion that I've never had before as I watch her body lay lifeless, but at the same time, I'm overjoyed that I haven't been caught yet and that my brother is alive. I glance at Candyce once again. She was going to kill me anyway, just like she did her flunky Jack.

All the tears that were prepared to come out seconds ago, dry up as more voices enter the room to speak to my aunt and uncle. My muscles grow tense as I slide down into my seat, and my heart misplaces the high it found over the news of Lug's survival because in a split second I realize I'd put him in more trouble. It's the cops, and they are sure to question him about me.

"I'm officer Williams and this is officer Patwall. We're the investigators for your nephew's shooting, and the first thing we want to let you know ma'am, sir, is that we are going to do everything we can to find out who shot your son. We'll have your nephew's eye witness

157

testimony, and although it's nightfall, he may know details about his shooter that will help us out," continues the officer. As the other officer cuts in, my thoughts spin out of control. I killed a man in his apartment.

"Shit!" I sit up in the car, but my mind is all a blur. But then, I hear my name.

"...Lisa Caldwell. We have to ask you if Luscious is related to Mrs. Caldwell because she's currently being tied to two homicides at her home. We...authorities have yet to contact her at all about what happened at her home which makes her our prime suspect. Do you have any information that you can give us?"

"Well..." Ma starts, but then Uncle Joe interrupts.

"They're brother and sister. What's going on at the house? I mean...I know only part but not all because the news..."

"I'm asking you to be honest with me. I know you love them both, but Lisa Caldwell needs to turn herself in. Therefore, if you have spoken to her, this could help out greatly. It may even be the reason for her brother being shot."

"What!" I scream from the car as I listen to what I consider bull shit. "Don't say shit, Uncle Joe!" I yell, but I know my voice is muted out. That's when my tears return. "I didn't get my brother shot. I didn't have anything to do with it. He needed money. Stupid fuckin' money!" My head falls onto the steering wheel in complete sorrow and anguish when there's a hard knock at my driver's side window. I jump over toward the gear shift, busting my elbow in the process. When I look up, there is some guy wearing a brown shirt and shorts asking for change. My nerves are shot, so without even thinking I frantically shout, "No! Get away from my window!"

"Well, forget you then," he says limping off while looking back at me. "All that money in the car, and you can't give me nothing…"

The bag! I glance to my side, and the bag of money is wide open. "Damn!" I roll the window down fast, grab a bundle and call him back to the car. "Wait!" Then, I lower my voice, "Come here…look. Take it but leave the parking lot and don't say a word about where you got it. Split it up. Go get a hotel and a good night's sleep. Sorry." I squeeze the money from the top of the window directly into his hands, and immediately, tears run down his eyes.

"You got to be my angel. You got to be. Lord, thank you. I ain't no addict, ma'am. I'm just down on my luck. I won't tell nobody, nobody. Thank you. I can buy me some clothes with all this and get an address. That's all I need! Bless you," he continues to talk and just to shut him up, I stuff another load of money into his hands, tell him to hide it and leave quickly. Soon, he's out of my sight and my focus goes back onto my uncle's words.

"Before he got shot, he called me," he stammers, "And he said that he was dropped off by Lisa earlier, you know, to get to his job on time. We talked about what was on the news, but it had just happened and I haven't seen her," he finally lies. "I haven't seen her. All Lug said is that she dropped him off at the firm… Smiths & Brothers. It was a secret that he'd let me in on that he had a job and all in his future field, you know, but we did talk about the news report…yeah, I'm gonna be honest, we did. Are you sure that Lisa committed a crime, officer, or do you just need her for other reasons…like just to question her about…?"

159

"We have reason to believe that Lisa herself killed two people in her home. It was either her or someone with her, but that's why we need her for questioning. There are things surrounding this whole morning that points to something being not quite right with your niece, and she herself may be in danger."

"Well, my niece didn't kill nobody! You hear me! You prove that she killed somebody, and I'll call your proof planted evidence, you hear me! Get out! Go find who shot my boy!" Ma screams, and the piercing of emotional pain shoots all the way through my soul. Vomit is already all over my pants and the car, so I open up the door to regurgitate again. It's all too much for me to handle, so I close the door back when I hear one of the officers call in for another officer to go by the firm to see if anyone could identify me on the scene or if anyone could get some surveillance.

"Ma'am, I'm going to leave now because I don't want to have to arrest you for hurling threats the wrong way. I'm doing my job. Sir, if you talk to her at any time, tell her to turn herself in because it's obvious she's running."

"Officer…I think she has my car."

"Joe! Joe, Joe, no!" Ma cries, but it's obvious that my know it all Uncle Joe isn't listening because he continues to talk which causes me to drive off immediately inside the car that will be trackable in moments.

"My wife said she stopped by when I wasn't at home asking to use my car to pick up some friends. She let her use the car, and we haven't seen her since."

Hearing those words come from Uncle Joe's mouth crush my entire spirit of freedom as I speed off on the road to nowhere, with no plan, a dead body and a bunch of money in that dead body's bag. Immediately, I think of how Candyce could have helped me along the way, and then I start second guessing myself. What if Nate didn't order her to kill me? What if she wasn't about to reach down in her bag for the gun to blow my brains out?

Smack is still over there sitting on Candyce's lap as if she's still alive. It's like she's waiting on her owner to get up and do her usual - pet and slob her down in the mouth like they're quirky lovers. Unfortunately, that's not going to happen.

"Not anymore, Smack. Not anymore. I had to do it, just like I had to kill your dumb ass Uncle Robert and his whore. I feel like all this stuff I did is self defense, Smack," I whine to her as I turn the corner onto a back road going to nowhere. "She was a fucking stranger in my home, stole my damn dinner, threw her clothes all over the place and then…my damn eye is black as hell from Robert's fist. His fist!" I wipe my eyes off and keep rambling. It's the only thing that I have to do that will keep me sane. As I drive near a pond, I contemplate driving over into it, but I know that would be a fail because I can swim. I would just swim myself out and be without a car, and what sense would that make to walk my ass around wet and wanted?

The streets are dark and for some odd reason, no one is outside. On this part of town, people stay outside at night, but there's nothing going on which makes me uneasy. Therefore, I slow the car down at the stop sign, making sure that I come to a complete stop before I turn the corner. I don't see any police officers, but as soon as I make the turn, something moves from the side of my eye. My foot slams onto the brake, and the car screeches near some woods.

"What the hell?" I whisper. My eyes strain in the darkness, but I dare not turn on any light inside the car for fear of someone recognizing me. "Smack," I call staring at her directly in her bushy face. "Come here, honey. Come to Aunt Lisa. Come on, baby." Smack doesn't move one paw, so I slowly lean over and look at Candyce with her hair covering her face just like I laid her in the seat. I then stare at her chest...and wait. Smack continues to wag her tail, but she's a dog. Dogs aren't stupid. Before staring at her chest for a complete minute, I reach over and dump the money out of the open bag, hoping to quickly grab the gun she used to kill Jack. As soon as I feel it, I yank my hand from the bag, and I sit there with it aimed at Candyce's still chest, my foot still on the brake. "Candyce if your ass is alive, you better move right now and call Nate. Tell him you're alive, or I'll finish this mother fucking job right now and dump your faking ass body in those woods!"

"Fuck you, Lisa," she answers turning her head slowly to face me, her bloody hair sticking to her face. "So now you're gonna shoot me, huh? Are your really gonna shoot me?" She says trying to move over so she can stare me directly in my face, but she grabs her neck in agony. "You just tried to fucking kill me anyway!" she screams in anger.

"Yeah," I state as my throat quivers. Candyce is my girl, but I'll try to kill her twice if I think she's coming for me. "There's no second guessing what you did to Jack back there because I saw it with my own two eyes. Don't act like I'm not a flunky, too. Shit just didn't go your way this time, right?" She doesn't answer, so I repeat myself but louder. "Right!" My hand fumbles the pistol so I grab it with two hands.

"I wasn't gonna kill you!" Candyce starts to weep, but I sit strongly in my seat ready to blast her to smithereens for those reach-and-call-my-bluff moves she's been making on me even while faking dead.

"I bet your ass wasn't," I respond out of breath and in disbelief. "The only reason why you didn't reach for the gun again is because your damn body is in no condition to move fast."

"Because of you! I need a doctor, so please get me to one. Just put me out…" she explains, reaching for the door knob.

"Hell no. If you open that door, I'm shooting. After that, then you can fall out. While you're still breathing though, I can't let you out of my sight." I look at her cell phone. "Now call Nate. Tell him that you're not dead and you need a car or the shit will fall out of his game like diarrhea. That's payback for wetting me up."

"Does it look like I can call him, Lisa, and for what? You're a murderer! I can barely see anything because you beat my eye in! It's all over the news, and that's what Nate told me on the phone. Something about you killed some people at your own house. It was Robert, wasn't it? Who else are you around here killing, you stupid psychopath!" she yells, frustrated because she can't do anything but lie there in pain while Smack tries to seal her head wounds. "You even have my dog licking my blood! What kind of animal are you, Lisa?" she cries. "I wasn't gonna kill you!"

All I can do is stare at her. It's like she's come back from the dead. Who on earth can survive a beat down to the head like I gave her but someone meant to be alive? I finally flick on the light in the car, only for a second, and I see that her face is mangled along with her head which has a huge devil's horn on the side. Although she looks like she should look after the whipping I gave her, I still ask the one simple question that she probably won't have an excuse for.

"If you weren't trying to set me up or shoot me, why didn't you hang up the phone, Candyce? So you could prove the job of killing me was done...like you're some fucking hitman?" I can tell that my question cuts through her like a knife, and after I see her expression, I flick the light back off. I knew it. I knew she was gonna kill me. There's nothing that she can say now, but I finally take a more relaxed position in my seat and listen to how she may try to whine herself out of this one.

"What do you mean?"

I just laugh. This heifer. I stare at her like she's a damn idiot and like I love to entertain them, and then she speaks again.

"Lisa, the phone was on because he wanted to hear if I was okay is all, especially after he heard the news. That's all. I swear that's it."

"So you just started rattling off all those questions at me, questions that can convict me later, especially if someone else hears me confess. Is that the type of thing you do to your friend? Are you supposed to air my secrets, Candyce?" She doesn't answer, so I put the car in park, lean over and knock her lightly in the head again with her own gun. "I tell you what you are. You're a lying ass. Here," I state handing her the phone. "Call Nate and put him on speaker phone. Tell him that you made it away from me and that you're still alive and you need a car delivered down the road."

"No, Lisa, please don't do that to me, please! He didn't tell me to kill you, so..."

I lift Smack up from her lap, and Candyce freezes. "If you love her, you'll do what I just said do. Now call him, and if you don't make up some dumb ass excuse like you normally do to get your way, Smack will probably die. Put him on speaker, Candyce.

"Where are we?" Candyce asks stupefied. I swear I will knock her upside the head again with her own dog if she doesn't stop acting so ignorant.

"This isn't dumb Jack you dumped back there in the ditch. It's me. Don't act stupid." I stretch the pistol closer to her head, and she starts to dial without anymore hesitation. I swear I'll smoke her like a cigarette if she doesn't play this off. Ashes to ashes and dust to dust. She presses speaker, and the phone starts to ring at the other end. Nate picks up on the second ring.

"Candyce?" he answers calmly. There isn't an ounce of fear in his voice at all.

"Yeah, it's me, baby. I'm still alive. Beat up to hell and back but that's all."

"Where are you?" he asks, still no anxiety in his voice.

"I'm down here, about four blocks from the fairgrounds next to the Waffle House." She glances up at me, and I glance at her dog. "I need a car, Nate. I'm stranded. Then I have to go turn her ass in for the murders because I think my car is at her house. She never told me where it was, but that's why the cops ended up at my spot earlier." She glances at me one more time, lifting her hand up to let me know that her turning me in is a part of her plan to get a car.

"Cops at your house? What!" Nate responds, straining his vocal chords. "Look, Candyce, baby," he continues, calming his voice down as he snaps his fingers in the background. "I'll send someone down there. Do you have the money with you or did she take it?"

"I actually have it, Nate, baby. She just dumped me out with everything and left. I can't walk around like this, but I need the cops off my back. That's why they need to see me like this…all busted up, so they can figure I've been kidnapped by the loon. I need a car. That way, the cops won't think twice about me because…" she pauses and looks at me. "We were friends."

"A car is on the way. So, you're gonna turn her in, huh? How will it work if after you turn her in, she turns me in?"

"She doesn't know your name, baby."

"She doesn't?"

"No…I never told her your name is Nathaniel Cylinders." She glances hopefully at Lisa whom she hopes takes a mental note of the name because she doesn't know if she'll live or die in the next hour. "She only knows Nate. That's it. As far as where you live, she can't retrace it if she tries."

"The car is black on black. One will follow the other. When you see the first man get out and get into the other car, you need to be ready to jump in and ride. In fifteen minutes, be across the street from the Waffle House at that run down bench. Sit down there. You should be alright. Don't lose that money, C, got it? If someone tries to sit beside you, don't let 'em."

"Yeah, yeah, I got it," she pauses, her voice quivering in fear as if she knows something is going to go wrong. Despite all her fear, I tap her leg to keep talking. "Nate, thank you, baby, and I love you. You know I love you, right?"

"Hell yeah I do. Why wouldn't you? My man is gonna take that cash from you, hold it for you so when you go to the cops, you won't have the shit on you? Do you understand?"

"Yeah."

"When the door comes open get in the car and my man will get out. Give him the money first and he'll get in the other car. This should take no more than 30 seconds. The cars aren't marked. Love you."

"Love you, too." They hang, up and I sit back, holding Smack by the tail as I start to drive again. The Waffle House is right down the street, and I know exactly what bench he was talking about. No one sits there because shootings happened there back to back. Anyone with sense knows to never sit on what is called the suicide bench, but tonight, my good friend Candyce is going to be on suicide watch.

"So his name is Nathaniel Cylinders?" I ask, but I don't expect Candyce to answer. Therefore, I give her my own plan. "That's a great plan, Candyce, but before you get out, I'm taking my half of the money. What's mine is mine. I'm no thief." I know it sounds stupid as hell, but I'm really not a thief. A reactive killer as of recent, but not a thief. "You might just try to get away with him but remember, if you take off in that car without me, Smack will be laying smack on that ground like some smack." Truth is, I'm just calling Candyce's bluff. I've never been offended in Smack. I really do love the dog, so I'm leaning on Candyce believing me based off of my prior killings…well, the ones that she knows about. "When I drop you off at the bench, I'm going around the block where I can see you through the trees. When I see you get in the car, you need to circle the block until you see this car. When you do, let the door swing open, and I'll jump in. You better remember that I have your loaded gun on Smack the whole time."

"Don't kill my baby, Lisa. Don't kill my baby," she cries, but her cries end soon as I pull up to the Waffle House. It's packed as usual, however, I don't wait on anyone to see how frantic I look, so I press on the gas to drop Candyce off at the suicide bench.

"Wait, I can't get out."

"Try your best because I can't get out either."

As I watch Candyce pull herself up by the door's handle, she pulls her hair back into a ponytail. Then she looks down at Smack with a crooked smile, and then the smile fades when she looks at me. Good thing I have on my sunglasses. I look away.

"What happened? That's the least you can tell me before you let me out. You fucked my hair and face up, so go on. Tell me."

I don't hesitate to tell her. What else can she do when I have the love of her life cradled in my arms with a pistol waiting to fire? Checking the road both ahead and behind me, I make the conversation quick. That's the least I can do although I'm shaken as fuck. I have to play like I'm hard as hell so my dear friend who has miraculously survived the attack won't try anything to save her own life.

"I caught Robert in bed with one of his girlfriends after they ate the dinner I cooked for him. I'd set the table and all, but when he got home, he beat my ass, hence my black and red eye. When I left, I decided to go back. That's when I caught him in bed, both their clothes off, and he told her that he loved her. I slit her throat, stabbed his ass up and then I left. I forgot some of the other stuff, but I went shopping for Smack some food. Then you called me on the road when I was pulling your car in the garage, saying you were being late. Then, when I got in, I had to make a run for it because the cops and everyone on the street was in front of my house. I left your car there and took my car elsewhere. Now, we're here and you're getting out to come pick me up in a different car." I turn my eyes back to look her in the face and her mouth is wider than an elephant's head. "Bye." I turn to face the road, ready to drive ahead. "I'll see you in twenty minutes." She hands me my sum of money and takes the left over in her bag. Then, she looks outside the window.

"This is suicide bench."

"Get out of the car!" I scream directly inside of her beat up face. I can even see traces of ash from the ashtray on her cheekbone as she stares at me like I'm not supposed to let her out at the bench. "What?" I yell. "It was your man's idea! Get out!"

"I love you, Smack. Mommy's coming to get you, okay, baby girl? Even your fucked up ass ex-aunt can't kill me," she curses me as she limps her half dead butt out of my car. When she shuts the door, I sense the fear in her body so I stay put even after she sits down. I start trying to count down ten minutes so she won't have to sit there alone, because even though I tried to kill her, I'm glad she's alive because it turns out that I need her at least for now.

As the time ticks by, I press on the gas causing the car to roll forward. Before I lose sight of Candyce, my heart softens. It's kind of weird because even though I tried to kill her because I swear she tried to kill me by Nate's orders, I still don't want anyone to kill her. Watching her look into the back windshield of my Uncle Joe's car that now has a small dent on its outside but a complete wreck on the inside, the phone rings. It's my Aunt Lyndi.

"Ma?" I pick it up while making a sharp turn. I toss Smack to the passenger's side seat and continue to drive, bumping the curb in the process.

"Lisa, Lisa baby, they know the make of the car. They say you really did kill a man and woman in your house. I saw your clothes baby, so I know it had to be self defense wasn't it baby because if it was, you can turn yourself in. You have to get out of that car though, honey…"

Ma is rambling. I can tell she's all alone where ever she is talking. I only imagine what she's going through right now, so I try to comfort her as best I can. Deep in my heart, I feel I have to tell her the complete truth in order for her to at least come to grips with things – accept them for what they are. As I turn the next corner to park in a good spot so that I can keep my eyes on Candyce as she sits there with her back turned to me, I begin revealing all of what happened back at my house and more to Ma.

"I never had migraines. I lied. Robert would beat me, and today when you saw me, my eye was black and red. The red on my clothes was from when I killed them, and the water is from where I tried to hose off." Candyce is still sitting there alive on the suicide bench. No car has showed up yet, so I continue to talk through Ma's heavy breathing and crying. She's weeping a lot now, but there's nothing I can do about it but allow it to drag my soul to hell because I feel like that's where I'm going because I still don't feel bad about killing Robert nor his girl.

"It was Robert and his girlfriend, Ma. After they ate all the dinner I made, they had sex in my bed, and then I walked in and killed them. It's self-defense."

"What?"

Before she continues to ramble in her sorrow, I wipe the tear that comes from my eye which is a result of her pain and re-state, "Self-defense. I was defending my marriage, my dinner and myself. Ma," my voice cracks as I finally let loose of my anger and face my hurt to someone else. "They nearly killed me on the inside! They may not have touched my body, but they tried to destroy me, Ma! You should see me, I mean…" I look down at my chest where my concealed heart is destroyed, looking worse than my face or Candyce's face put together. "Look at me really, Ma! I didn't let you see me because you wouldn't have recognized anything about me. He took everything from me for years, so the only way I could get some life back inside me is to take his. At least I have something now, right, Ma? So see," I begin to cry. "It really is self defense. I have to go now, Ma. Tell Lug that I'm okay - that I'm taking care of everything - and tell Uncle Joe I said his car is fucked up now, so thanks for ratting me out. Besides that, I'm not in the car anymore. I love you." I hang up and watch as a black car drives up in front of Candyce while another one pulls up right beside her.

I sit up in my chair so that I can monitor the situation as Candyce moves from suicide bench as fast as she can. Then I watch as she slides into the driver's seat before shutting the door. The next thing I watch is what

171

looks like a man get out on the passenger's side and get into the driver's side of the other car, and then they take off. I breathe a sigh of relief and start trying to gather up as many things as I can from the car that was left into my arms along with Smack. When I stare back up at the car, it's still not moving.

"What?" I ask aloud, unsettled by things not going as I thought they would. Therefore, I call her from my cell. As it rings, it gets interrupted by the voicemail message. My stomach plummets to my ass. "Candyce?" I call under my breath, but then I hang up the phone as I stare at the black car simply sitting there directly at suicide bench. "Stay right here, Smack."

I toss Smack over onto the passenger's seat, and then look around. No one is outside on this side of the block, and I have a straight shot to suicide bench if I cut through the two yards that separate me from it and Candyce. In desperate need of another car, I hop out of Uncle Joe's wagon and haul my terrified butt into the first backyard. The grass is in need of a serious cut because the weeds are whipping at my shin bone beneath my pants. By the time I get to the next yard, it's lined with a wire fence on both sides, but there's a gap in between them. As I make my way through, sliding sideways as fast as possible, a bull dog comes charging my way, and I fall back against the other fence, ripping my shirt as I continue to struggle my way past the mad mut.

"Ouch! My back!" I yelp and lift up off the fence, but when I do, the bull dog bites at my arm, ripping through some skin. I want to yell, but I groan instead and pull my arm fiercely away from his jaws. At this point, I lean on the other fence behind me, no matter how scarred up my back gets, and keep going.

172

The outside of my arm is dripping so much blood that if I didn't know any better, I would've thought the crazed dog hit an artery. The bull dog follows me all the way to the other side of the fence, and when I get through to the other side, I drop to the ground. Squeezing my arm doesn't help the pain, so as soon as I know the coast is still clear, I bolt to the car, praying that the door is open. The first time I pull on the latch, the door doesn't open, so I continue yanking, not only because I need the car, but because I'm a bloody, painful mess outside where a bunch of people have already heard of the fiasco I drummed up this morning via all the news stations. Finally the door opens, but a limp and gasping for air Candyce falls out of the car.

"No, no, no!" I moan as I shift my entire body up underneath her upper body which is leaning up against the car, and then I forcefully shove her over. Her body lifelessly falls, her head hitting the passenger's side seat. My arm throbs as I sit a portion of my body on the seat and with a giant heave, use all my body weight, which isn't that much, to get Candyce over the gear far enough so I can get the car in drive. I hear Candyce struggling to breathe, but I can't help her right now because I have to get off this street. Pulling the car away from the suicide bench, I drive carefully around the corner while the blood from my arm drips everywhere. Just as soon as I lose sight of the people on the street, I punch on the gas until I make it back to my Uncle Joe's car. Candyce's body has already slumped down even further onto the seat which leads me to think she's been shot and killed.

As soon as I stop the car, I jump out, open up Uncle Joe's car door, grab Smack, and pop the trunk. All of Jack's and Lisa's luggage are inside, so I pull it out and shove it in the trunk of this black unmarked car. My uncle keeps some old license plates on his back windshield, so I take two and sit one of them on the back window just in case. The cops aren't looking for this black car so I don't really want anyone pulling me over for tags. Sure, they still could pull me over, but what the heck? Don't they have better things to do today like find me?

It only takes me one minute tops to get the luggage piled in because they didn't have much. I jump in my uncle's back seat to grab any other loose stuff that ties them to me, and I also look in the front seat. Besides the vomit, it's clean, so I rush into the unmarked-thanks-to-Nate car and drive off. Then I notice that I forgot to check on Candyce. I stop the car, lean over and check her pulse. She's dead. I should have figured because Smack is in the back seat sniffing her and running back to the window over and over again like she's trying to get help. Before I start driving again, I reach over and touch her chest and stomach. That's when I feel the blood from the entry wound coming from her abdomen. Nate had her shot and killed, plus he took the rest of the money. I sit back up.

"At least he thinks I'm long gone." One down. I can't feel too bad with Candyce lying there next to me dead. I already thought she was dead once earlier today, but besides that, she can say what she wanted to say, she was going to blow my brains out. I press on the gas and continue driving.

Chapter 23

"We're going to have to place you under arrest. You have the right to remain silent…" the officer continues to read out Miranda rights to Lug as he lies inside the hospital bed wounded by a gunshot to his back.

"What?" he asks, but gets no response until another officer enters the hospital room.

"Do you have anything to say about the dead man found inside your apartment, Mr. Caldwell? We obtained a warrant to search in and around your premises after finding out through a co-worker that you were actually on the phone with your sister right before you left your job. This same co-worker stated that you were possibly on your way home after finding out your sister was wanted for questioning about the homicides at her address. You were said to have lied and said you were sick in order to leave …"

"I didn't kill anybody!"

"What's going on in here? Leave my nephew alone! Can't you see he's been shot? Leave him alone!" Lyndi reaches over about to grab the police officer, however, Joe comes in just in time to restrain her and apologize to the officers.

"She's distraught right now, so will you please forgive her?" he stammers as he tries to contain Lyndi who watches in sorrow as her nephew is placed in handcuffs. "What's going on, officer?" he asks frustrated. "It seems it's just one thing after another, so can you please…"

The officer raises his hand up and starts to talk when Joe falls quiet. "Upon one of our officers going into your nephew's apartment, there was a man found murdered on the floor. His throat had been cut all the way open, according to officers on the scene, and this is why we must make this arrest. Right now, the only thing I need to ask you two is the location of Lisa Caldwell if you know anything at all about what's going on being that she's riding around in your car?"

"Lug, what is this about? You know anything about somebody dead in your apartment?" Joe asks sternly before getting put out of the room. Lug doesn't answer. He simply stares upward at the ceiling, refusing to fight with his handcuffs as two tears drift down his cheeks. His lips quiver as he struggles to hold back his sorrow as he copes with the horrible truth all alone while his family and the cops look back at him like he may be a stone cold killer. He does this all for the sake of his older sister and deceased mother who always told them to stick together no matter what.

In the moments that follow as his Aunt Lyndi is escorted out of the room along with his Uncle Joe, Lug imagines his Aunt Lyndi as his mom looking back at him fighting and telling him to keep quiet, to stick by his sister just like she's always stuck by him. He continues to think back to his mom forcing them to share everything until it became second nature. If one had more money in the piggy bank, the other would always ask if the other needed anything. That was and still is the only way. This time, Lug knows without question that Lisa needs him, and because of how he was raised, he doesn't know how to not be on Lisa's side, for right or for wrong.

The door slams to take him out of his trance, and his eyes move from the ceiling to another officer now sitting in front of him on the arm of a recliner. The man wears a suit, the stuffy kind that may be worn about twice a week just to make the time go by. His voice when he speaks is one of the deepest, almost threatening kind, but his laid back demeanor cancels the voice out.

"Luscious, I'm Detective Bolden. I'm going to go ahead and cut to the chase. We know that you went back to your apartment when you left work suddenly," he clears his throat to continue. "Actually, it looks like it was your first day as a law student intern, so you already know the law, am I right?"

Lug darts his eyes away from him, but then finds the courage to stare him back in the face but without saying a word. Lug sure does know the law, and the one thing he is certain of is that there is no proof that he killed Jimmy. There is absolutely no proof, especially when the coroner says the time of death which he hopes will match more with the time he was at work.

"No answer, huh? Invoking the fifth amendment, I see. Well look, Luscious Caldwell. I also know your sister dropped you off at work, so either you both killed that poor man together, you did it before you left or when you got back. The fact is that the man is lying on your floor in a bunch of blood. As a matter of fact, someone even saw you get out of the car when you got to the apartment."

Luscious' poker face is classic, strong and unaffected by the round of assumptions and questions. No matter what, there's nothing the detective can say to make him throw the wrap on his sister nor himself. A lawyer is the most Lug can and will say.

"Where's my lawyer?"

"You know you're under arrest for the murder?"

"Where's my lawyer?"

"You can either tell me now or…"

"I said where's my fucking lawyer?" Lug finally explodes in a fit of rage that doesn't stun the detective at all.

"We'll get you one," he smiles. "We'll get you one." Then he gets up and walks out the room, shaking his head.

Lug watches as the door closes behind the detective while the only sound he hears afterwards is his aunt screaming madly in the hallway. His emotions overwhelm him, and then he finally lets it all out by repeatedly hollering so loudly that nurses are ordered inside to give him a dose of intravenous drugs to put him to sleep.

Chapter 24

The night has grown quiet as I continue to drive down to the beach. No one knows where I am nor can they say what I'm driving. It's just me and Smack technically because even though Candyce's body is right here beside us, her spirit is long gone. This is the reason why I'm going to the edge of the water tonight. I'm going to go to the most deserted part of the beach I know about and let her float away. Her luggage is in the back, so I'll tie it around her ankle.

When I get to the spot that I used to come to with an old boyfriend of mine, the one that I should have married, I pull up really close to the water. It's still, just like when we would come out with each other together. Even the scent of the water is the same.

"Smack, go pee," I say to her as she jumps from the car and starts to turn around in circles and sniff until she finally finds the proper spot for her to release. "I was right. No one would be out here." Without anymore delay, I walk over to the other side of the car to get my late best friend, or the person I thought would never plan to harm me. As I pull Candyce out onto the ground, I wonder if I went overboard with her, but then I think I'm really not the one who killed her like I thought I did. Either way, she knows too much, and just like Nate had to get rid of her, so do I- body and all for good if I want to continue driving around in this car.

I accidentally trip over Candyce's dead arm as I walk to the trunk. The trees sway in the light breeze from one side to the other around the water. My nerves are frazzled, so I feel I have to explain myself before dumping her. "They fucked me over, so I had to do the same to them. Candyce," I continue, glancing over at her as I pull her luggage out, "we aren't the same at all. I reacted, and you set the shit up. I won't feel bad about my kills. They just happened. I'm nothing like you because I didn't plan the shit." Then, I throw the luggage on the ground. "I had no choice! Your ass would have been alive, too, if you would have just minded your damn business!" Falling to the ground to open the luggage in search of a belt, from the side of my eye, Candyce lies there with her mouth open and eyes now shut, her corpse looking like a terrible hang over. I grin slightly as I recall when she was so loaded with alcohol and fogged up with marijuana after a party that she actually crawled up underneath my car to go to sleep. Robert was ticked off with me when I got home so late, and he didn't believe my honesty about having to look for her all over the club house until about one-thirty in the morning when I got inside my car. The only thing that prevented me from running her over was the fact that when I got inside my car, I looked down after stepping on her finger. Of course, she didn't feel it. I had to pull her out from underneath the car and head home. She recovered quite well. It was me who got a broken arm. I survived.

After finding the belt, I zip the luggage back up and tie one end of the belt to the luggage's handle and the other end to her ankle. Candyce always wears these chain type belts, and for this purpose, it works out well.

"You should have never tried to shoot me. You're my friend, not foe. Nate messed everything up…well," I state, pulling the belt around her ankle as tightly as I can, "it ended up working out fine for me so far. You know something, Candyce?" I ask, sitting down on the ground next to her feet. "Robert deserved to die. I never deserved anything I got from him. I took his beatings and still loved him. I took his cheating ass as he was, but that last time, he asked for that shit." I stand up from the ground and start to haul her toward the water. My feet dig into the sand as I stumble and fall over twice just getting her to the edge of the lake. "And here I go having to get wet again. Dang…wait."

I drop her upper body to grab a change of clothes from her bag along with some of her shoes that I know won't fit. I'll wear them anyway. It amazes me how our clothes fit each other but our feet are total strangers – mine are narrow and hers are wide and a size up. She has a pretty awesome selection for the trip to Jamaica. I even find one outfit with the tag still on, so that's the one I take. Undressing, I continue to scan this empty small and secluded section of the beach until I know that the outfit fits me perfectly. I take it back off so it won't get dirty and lay it on the car. Then, I toss the outfit that I just took off into the luggage. "Good deal," I sigh. "I can do this naked, with just my underwear on."

Going back to grab her legs, Smack jogs back over to me in a sad weep. "She's going to be okay. Just going for a swim. Consider me your new mom from here on out, okay, baby. She did me dirty, and she knows it." As my feet touch the water, I drag Candyce in. Her head lands at the tip of the water, and that's when I reach for the luggage to pull it into the water. Not knowing when the land underneath my feet will disappear, I walk slowly, careful to go one foot at a time out into the water until I feel a dip. Then, I place the luggage down in the water as Candyce's body floats along. Giving the luggage a large kick and then yanking the belt sends Candyce's corpse sinking downward. By the time day breaks, she should be long gone.

"Naked I stand, Smack, and divided we all go. Come on." I rush back to the car to put on the clothes, but then I remember Lug's stolen credit cards and ID's.

181

Opening the car door, I fumble through all the items that I grabbed and tossed inside until I found the cards in the plastic bag. I toss them into the water as well. "Be free, Lug. Be free."

My phone rings, but I ignore it. I don't want to pick the phone up out here, so I jump back in the car and drive away. Smack looks hungry, so I have to find her something to eat and fast because she's gone without food all day just about, just like I have. It's only been my adrenaline that's kept me going. Now that I have cash money on me, I can pull up to a drive-thru out here somewhere.

My phone rings once again when I get on the interstate, and it's Ma. I want to be as far away from where I dumped Candyce's body as possible before I answer the phone. I don't know how cell phones work, but whatever. Just because it's ringing, it may have already picked up my whereabouts.

"Hello?" I can't hear. "Hello?" I repeat.

"Lisa! Lisa, baby, they got your brother. He's gonna be okay but they got him," she hollers into the phone, nearly deafening my ear. I put her on speaker as my heart begins to thump rapidly once more.

"Who got him, Ma?"

"The cops! They said a dead man was in his apartment, and he's going to prison. Said they asked some girl at the job, and I don't know what's going on but your ass better start talking right now! Lug ain't no killer, and you aren't either, Lisa, I don't care what you say! You're covering for someone, baby, because you're not a killer."

My heart skips as I think of Lug in the hospital surrounded by cops, and I shout, without thinking, "I killed him! It was me, I did it, and Lug didn't even know! I killed them all, Ma! Just tell them to leave my brother alone. Leave him alone." The interstate becomes a tunnel to me as I sink into a massive nightmare. I see nothing but black despite the lights from various hotels and car dealerships around me. At the end of the tunnel, I imagine my brother in prison behind my killing in his apartment when he had nothing to do with it, and I cringe so bad until I almost swerve off the highway. A big eighteen wheeler blows its loud horn to get me back on track as he leans out his window to flick me off for the finale.

Ma is too busy crying in the background for me to stop her, so I just angrily repeat what I told her earlier along with the part I left out about Lug's apartment. There's nothing else for me to do. Maybe, if I scream it at the top of my lungs, she'll finally accept the ugly facts about me. "He used to beat me, Ma! There are no migraines, and when I came to your house earlier, all that I told you was a lie. I'd killed them." When I say that word killed, she wails even louder but I keep going, hoping that something I say will force her into acceptance of the fact that I took the lives of some people who for the most part, to me, deserved it. "He brought a woman in my house, Ma... just like I told you... ate my dinner and slept with her in my bed after he sent me out of the house with a black and red eye. I fuckin' cooked him that meal and he dragged a dirt bag bitch into my house and ate my food and then he had the nerve to tell her that he loves her." My voice cracks just saying it, but I repeat what I say just to let it sink into my pores once more. The more it sinks in, the less I feel remorse. " '*I love you*' he said to her, snuggled up in my sheets. So...I slit her throat and stabbed him to death. Ma," I recall as tears rip the pain into my cheeks,

"That's the reason he hated me. That right there. All that time I thought I was doing some shit wrong! It was him. He was fuckin' other women and was hitting me because I wasn't them! So fuck his dead ass."

I turn off of the interstate while Ma is still crying on the phone, but I continue. I know what I have to do now. "Lug didn't kill that man. When I dropped Lug off, I took his bike back to his apartment because, as everyone knows already, I have a key to his place. I went in to think about everything, and when I got ready to leave, I ran into a man named Jimmy. He'd seen the news. So, instead of answering his questions when he stepped in front of me, I pulled a knife and then slit his throat. Ma, I didn't plan it. I'm sorry, Ma," I cry, "I really am. I couldn't allow myself to get caught. I didn't even think Lug would get popped for it because he was at work. It's just that he would have turned me in, Ma! I still had things to do…I had to pick up my girl, and I just didn't know what to do because I had no money…and at that time nobody really knew. Nobody knew about Robert because it just happened!"

"No, child, no! Your mom would…"

"Ma? My real mom? She would have done the same thing if dad fucked around on her. I just know it! Your own sister would have took him out because she would have gotten just as angry as I am."

"You shut up! Just shut up! You came in my house, got my clothes to wear after a bald faced lie, took our car and got blood on everything. What are we supposed to do now, baby? As God is my witness, I tried to do all I can," she cries, deeply wounded by my actions which is why I interject again because I don't want her to blame herself.

"And I thank God for you, Ma. You didn't do this."
I fall silent until I get the courage to blame myself although
I truly don't feel at all like I'm to blame for most of it. "I
did. And Mom didn't do this either. I did. I'll fix it, too.
There's no sense in both of us...me and Lug...going to jail.
I'm gonna fix it. Lug needs some money, Ma. I need you
to get it for him, and trust me that he's not going to jail
over this. The money you need to get for him is gonna be
stashed at that tree you, me and Lug planted at mom's
grave. It'll be at her head under the dirt. Go get it tonight.
Lug is broke, but this will help him get his life together
much faster, become a lawyer easier. Got it, Ma?"

"Child, please..." she pleads.

"I'm not a child, Ma!" I wipe my eyes. "I wish I
was though. I really wish I was. It's too late. Just go get
the money. It's all I have for Lug left, and it's clean." I
hang up and turn off the road toward the cemetery to see
my real mom one last time.

As I turn into the cemetery, it's not hard to find
where she's buried even though it's extremely dark. We all
went to the store one day to purchase an Evergreen, and we
even got special permission from the cemetery owners to
plant the tree right there at the head of her grave.
Periodically, I would come and place chimes or notes on
the limbs of the tree, however, this time, it will be money.

I race the car right up to my mom's grave, and then
I kiss the dirt that covers her after jumping from the car. I
hug the ground just like it's her while reading her
tombstone – *I'm not dead, just passed over into God's
arms*. Five years before her unexpected death, she gave her
life to Jesus. It was a moment that I remember all too
clearly because she told me and Lug that it was the best
decision of her life. She said that she was finally able to let

go and let God with everything, including her illness. Cancer took her, but she would tell us that to be absent from the body is to be present with the Lord. That's all I needed to know to keep living…is that she is still present, present with the Lord. As for me right now, I don't know what God thinks of me. If I ask my mom, she would have told me that He still forgives those who repent. That's the thing…I haven't repented because God reads the heart, and He knows I would be lying.

"Momma, I'm so sorry. I know you want more for me than what you see me doing right now. I couldn't control it," I state quietly as I dig with my fingers through the dirt in an attempt to carve a hole in the ground. My nails gather gobs of dirt, and although my fingers are starting to hurt, I continue to dig as hard as I can to break all the roots of the grass and rock that lies beneath the surface. A bug runs across my hand, but I don't flinch because I feel like the only one out here to fear is myself. If that bug knew better, he won't cross my hand again. It may just die. "Momma, I just got tired, you know? I got tired of hiding. Do you see my eye? I think I might have lost my mind, Mom, but it's too late. It's just too late. Keep this here for, Lug." I get the money and layer it into the hole so that my Aunt Lyndi can see it. "It's not a whole bunch but it will help Lug get back on his feet and keep a roof over his head. You know how he likes to be independent and all, pretend like he has it all together. Aunt Lyndi will be coming to get it for him, and I have to go clear his name. I'll be okay, Momma. I love you." I kiss the ground again where she lay and then leave to a ringing phone which I don't answer when I get into the car.

Instead, I find a pen and a scrap piece of paper and write in big bold letters – *YOUR CAR IS A WRECK, BUT WORKING FINE. IT'S ON THE SAME BLOCK AS SUICIDE BENCH. LOVE YOU, MA, AND THANKS A*

LOT UNCLE JOE. I STILL LOVE YOU THOUGH. I get out of the car and go to put the note underneath the stacks of cash. Before I stand back up, a car comes speeding through the cemetery. My adrenaline flows like fire, and my feet hit the dirt as fast as they can. Before I can get into the car good and get the door closed, the car is blocking my way out. There's nothing in front of me but woods, so I jump out of the car and start to run for my life, not knowing who it is behind me. I can hear Smack running behind me as fast as she can go, until she eventually passes me.

"Lisa! Lisa!"

I continue to run, not identifying the voice that calls me. All I know is that my freedom is at stake, and there is no one under the law that will hear my side without seeing me as absolutely nothing more than a criminal. Hell, my own uncle sold me out.

"Lisa!" the person calls, grabbing my arm as I dive into the bushes kicking and screaming to get loose. No matter how hard I fight, the unknown man is overtaking me and my ferocious battle. When he grabs both my legs, I immediately become terrified thinking that he is about to arrest me or worse…rape me. There's a heavy limb on the ground beside me, so with all the strength I can muster, I lift it and swing. He drops my legs and falls backwards, but as I try to scramble myself up to my feet, he jumps on top of me, holding my hands down atop my body.

"Lisa!"

"No!" I scream, but when I feel his body no longer moving, only holding me still, I open my eyes to stare him in the face. "What?" I ask quietly, more calm yet confused as I look back at the other half of my birth. It's my father.

He doesn't look at all the same anymore, but maybe it's because of the darkness.

In the background, Smack is barking nonstop as the man I know as my father who left my mother and us a long time ago stares back in my face. He lets me go. Yes, this is my father. He just looks older and desperate, much different than the younger, confident man I remember. His face reminds me of the time he saw me fall on my bike near the gutter when I was only seven years old. He rushed over, much like he did just now, fell to the ground and tackled me at the leg before I rolled all the way inside.

"Daddy?" I scoot backwards and tears start falling down my face. "How did you know I was here? You live here? You live here?" I ask, shoving my finger into the ground.

"Yeah...yes, Lisa. It's me," he stammers. "I moved back a couple months ago. Just a couple months. Your Uncle Joe is the only one that knew about the move, not even your Aunt Lyndi. He's the one who called me, not even five minutes ago and told me you were close by."

"Get the fuck off me!" I kick him in his stomach, at least I try, but he blocks it. "You're a liar! You left us! You didn't even come back to see us when mom died. You ain't shit!" I haul off to hit him in the face, but he grabs my arm. I start to cry. "We didn't even need you. We made it! You see! Look at me," I scream standing to my feet, proud of the woman whom I've become, despite all I've been through.

"You don't look like you're doing too good, Lisa, honey," he responds with a sad countenance, desiring to help his child in any way he can.

"I don't look too good? What? You think you can help me?" I return fire in absolute shock. "Me? Where the hell were you when Robert was breaking in my face? Is that why you say I don't look too good? This is what he did to me!" I pull my eye apart, indifferent of the pain it causes. "Look at it! You see it? And where were you?" I shout as close to his face as I can get. "Where? Fucking some other woman and taking care of her family? Is that why you left us, to take care of other fucking people?"

"Listen to me!" he interjects, grabbing my shoulders like I'm a rag doll, but I break away.

"Fuck you, daddy! You ain't never helped me one day in my life except when I nearly fell in that damn gutter," I cry. "It's too late now. It's too late! I fell in it this time, daddy. I fell, and you can't save me."

"Come on now, Lisa. I'm gonna try. I owe you that, and I'm sorry for everything I've done to you by not being there for you." He puts his hand over my black eye. "Robert…he hit you? He would beat you?"

I'm shocked that he even knows my husband's name. "And yeah…so what! Yeah, he did it last night, and this morning I killed him." I step away from my father, and look him straight in the eyes. "Why can't a man just love me? Not even you, daddy. I killed him and the woman he was laying up with in *my* bed. Then later I killed someone else at Lug's place. Even another friend of mine is dead. Now, tell me how proud you are of me, dad."

Tears stream down his face like a sobbing toddler, but I refuse to cry anymore in his face. Although he wasn't there with me, I still blame him for half of all my troubles. I realized late in life that the whole reason why I tried to prove myself to Robert or forgive him for any and everything was because of the absence of the man standing in front of me – my father. By the time I tried to change that about myself, it was so hard that I couldn't do it in time. When I did come back to at least stand my ground and proclaim my own defense, look what happened. I murdered him.

"I'm still proud of you, Lisa. You're my little girl, and you'll always be my good little girl. I failed you, baby. I would drive by your house sometimes to try to get a look at you when I moved back, but I would never stop the car. I happened to run into your Uncle Joe one day in passing at a gas station. He swore he would give me time to approach you, but I didn't know this would happen. That's why he called me to tell me you were on your way here. He wanted me to see you because he and God are the only ones who know my intent."

"Send Lug to school," I interject because what he calls his intent is a couple of days too late for me. "I put some money there for Lug. Aunt Lyndi is on her way to get it. Help him get his law degree because he needs money."

"I need to help you…"

"No, I'm done!" I walk off, heading back toward the car, but then I turn back to tell him one more thing. "I found my own way out of at least one gutter. I found out how to not take shit off any man anymore…including your bullshit."

I enter the car, Smack jumping in right after me, and when I turn on the car lights, I see my father standing there at the tip of the woods, looking at me. I thought I'd never see him again. As a matter of fact, I thought he might have even been dead when he didn't come to mom's funeral. An overwhelming sense of love suddenly comes over me, and instead of driving off like anger intended for me to do, I exit the car again and run toward him. It's amazing to me how he opens his arms all the way up after I said all that I said to him, and when I jump into his arms, he catches me and doesn't let me go.

"I love you, daddy," I cry. The tears just keep coming, and all my rage disappears. All daddy does is cry on my shoulder and I on his. It is at this moment that I don't care that he left. I don't even care about what he's ever not done throughout my life. I only care that he came to try and rescue me, that he's here now, and I'm in love with seeing him one more time. He is who was missing from my life, and I'm so happy, despite it all, that he's back. He's really back.

He pulls me from his shoulders, and I back away, still holding on to him like he's about to take off and never come back again. A tremendous weight drifts from my body as I finally feel like I have someone in my corner, not screaming and shouting at me, looking for answers to something they can't possibly understand.

"I know you feel like you need to run, baby girl, but…"

"I do," I quickly interject, wiping my face from all the tears. "I do have to run. I have something that I have to do. Just know that I never stopped loving you, dad." I crack a weak smile. "I'm pissed…I was pissed off a lot… but I love you. Thanks for coming to try and save me from this gutter, but I have to survive this one on my own." I kiss him on his cheek and as I back away, I visibly watch sorrow engulf his body. Quickly, I turn around, get back into the car and leave. This time, I leave the car lights off until I am far away from him. I don't even look back in the rear view mirror. Goodbye, dad.

Driving down the road, my mind is cluttered with thoughts of me and dad. From the time I recognized it was him trying to pull me out from the woods, my whole life seems to have changed. I want to take everything back immediately - not kill anyone - just to have the time I need to get to know him again, to have the time for Lug to bond with him as well, but everything is so wrong. There's absolutely nothing that I can do about it either.

My face in the rear view mirror looks like a woman, wife, widow, sister, daughter and a murderer, except to anyone looking at me with fresh eyes, murderer would be the last thing to describe me in their minds. I look nothing like one. I find a gas station and decide to walk inside. Pulling into the station, I just want to gather the feeling for one of the last free moments of my life to carve out a calm conversation, make a person laugh, spin around in search of the right pack of gum…just do common things that I may never get to do again once the cops stop me. I'm no longer on the run. That's over now that Lug is in trouble, and I have to get him off. I'm really just playing a waiting game, but I want my arrest to be by choice and on my own terms.

When I enter the gas station, it's nearly empty. I remove my sunglasses. There's a trash can to my right, so I toss them over inside. I'm tired of hiding, not only from the reality of my face, but the reality of my present and soon to be future. I don't care even if someone inside the gas station recognizes me. I just want to be normal, the way I was when I wasn't married to Robert - just a single lady, living, loving and being me. I haven't been that in so long.

Walking across the station, there's a man standing up next to the coolers, so that's where I go. I took only twenty dollars out of the cash because I figure that's all I need. When I reach the cooler, I sneak a peek at the gentleman beside me, and he doesn't have on a wedding ring, a possible athlete because his muscles bulge like they need to be held on to, and he has a nice smile.

"How ya doing? Are you alright?"

"Yeah, I'm fine. I just need to get into that same cooler after you're done," I respond.

"I haven't made up my mind yet, so feel free." He glances at my black eye. "You might need to see about that though."

"About what?" I ask, reaching inside the cooler to get a not so fresh tea as I pretend I have no idea what he's talking about. I generally brew my tea, however, this will work for the occasion.

"Your eye. It's bloodshot and bruised. Don't tell me you got into a fight or your man hit you."

I shut the door of the cooler, open my tea and answer him, heaven bent on not telling one lie. "Yeah, it wasn't much of a fight. He knocked me right upside my head," I laugh.

"What's so funny, though?" he asks. "Getting hit? Is that funny to you? No, sis, that's serious stuff."

"I know, but I had to learn," I pause, "I had to learn that I shouldn't take that crap anymore, and that's why I'm out here this late at night trying to relax and figure things out for myself."

"Good for you. Excuse me." He leans in to get the same exact drink I picked up. "Looks good. Think I might try one."

"It's better hot."

"Yeah?"

"Yeah, really."

"I'm not much of a hot tea drinker."

"You should try it sometime. Green tea is a favorite of mine, caffeinated or not. It's super good for you." I take a big swallow of my drink, not too concerned about drinking before paying because I'm headed to the big house anyway.

"Well, I'm out of here. Take care of yourself. Don't let a man go upside your head anymore, okay? Press charges. Here's my number." He pulls out a card with his name on it. "Officer Dellis."

The tea loses its way across my throat, and I start to strangle. I really can't breathe, so I try and gasp for air as I grab the handle of the cooler. Unfortunately, I'm in such a fight for air that I inadvertently yank the thing open, knocking myself to the floor after losing balance.

"Oh damn, you okay?" My eyes catch a glimpse of his bottled tea hitting the floor and him reaching around me to bang the tea from my air-blocked lungs.

I can't answer him as I struggle to catch my breath while zooming in on the card that has already dropped to the floor. Officer damn Dellis. He's a cop! While I'm struggling, I manage to scoot backwards slowly, but instead of him allowing me to help myself, he scoots with me. Therefore, the last thing I do is hold my hand up in the air and shake it to signify to him that I'm okay. That's when he backs up.

"You got it? You sure?" he asks extremely concerned.

Finally able to speak, I answer, "Yeah. Thanks," I sigh, taking in a deep breath. "You better get going."

"Alright. Give me a call sometime, and don't let that man hit you again."

With my head down, I respond, "He won't. Trust me."

"Glad you decided to leave. Take care." He walks away after getting his drink from the floor. I watch behind the shelf as he goes to the counter, pays for his drink and walks out the door.

Peering out of the window, I see that the car he gets into isn't a police car, however, I'm still unsettled about the whole thing. So much for my chill time before I serve time. I should just be glad he didn't arrest me for drinking from the tea bottle before buying it.

"Damn." I quickly pull out the money I have to pay for the tea and approach the counter slowly. I want some chewing gum and chocolate candy, so I stroll to the candy aisle to search for what looks good. As I search, another employee comes from the back, a male. Good, I think. I haven't had the opportunity to freely talk to a man since the cop left, and now I have another shot. Black eye or not, I need the time.

"I got this. Go ahead and break. Your mom sounded like she needed to talk to you about something."

"Are you sure?" the female attendant asks.

"If I wasn't sure, I wouldn't be out here. Bounce," he responds as he pulls up a stool to sit at the register. He's a young guy, about Lug's age, but he wears a huge amount of confidence on his shoulders as he looks out at the gas pumps to be sure everything is okay outside. When I walk to the counter with the items, I try to detract attention from my terrible hair and black eye by flaunting what I have pertaining to the rest of my body in Candyce's outfit.

"Hi." I put my items on the counter.

"I see you drank just about all the tea, so thanks for not tossing it," he laughs, and I laugh along with him. "I would have. You need to get some of that ice out there for that eye though. Damn," he continues. "Did you get some gas or are you getting ready to get some?"

"No, and my eye will be alright. Is it always this quiet at this gas station? It may be late, but it's still kind of early... for business, I mean."

"It's always like this. This isn't exactly the city. It's right on the outside of it."

"Well, sorry to bother you if it's lounging time."

"No, you're good. I'm out of here in about five minutes. Had to send her back there, but when she gets out, I'm gone. Locking up the entrance so you just made it." He hands me my change.

"Good. I hate standing out at that small window at gas stations, but I understand why you have to do that."

"Yeah, there's some crazy ass people out here. Hate to do it, but we have to."

After those words come from his mouth, I feel like a stranger in my own skin. I used to be such a beautiful

196

person, but when I glance at the reflection in the glass door, I am one of those crazy ass people…at least to others. They just don't know my story.

"See ya."

"Alright now," the guy says, totally uninterested in me, I can tell. "Be careful out there."

I don't respond. Instead I just walk out with my merchandise in my hand. The door closes behind me, and as soon as it does, I notice the guy that was pounding my back to try and save my life, come jogging up to the door right in front of me.

"We meet again!" he says with a smile on his face. "I think I forgot something," he says to me, looking directly in my face as if he's never seen me before.

"I see. Well, excuse me," I respond, not wanting him staring back in my face for only God knows how long. I pop some gum inside my mouth as he walks behind me, and suddenly my bag falls from my hand. Who I know as Officer Dellis grabs my right arm and pulls it behind my back, and the next thing I know is that I'm on the ground.

"Hey, man, hey, get back!" I hear the male attendant run out of the store, but as I lie on the ground, I watch his feet retreat when the officer reveals his identity.

"I'm an officer of the law. Get back inside and lock your doors. Give me your other hand, Lisa. You're under arrest."

I don't even cry. I just accept my fate. As he lifts me up, I watch Smack jumping up and down inside the car, so I glance back at the officer who is on his cell phone calling what I assume is his back up.

"My dog Smack is in the car. Someone has to take care of Smack. She really needs to eat. Can you please…"

"Don't worry about the dog, Lisa Caldwell. That is your name right? We will take care of the dog. Do you realize that we've been looking for you all day?"

I refuse to answer.

"You're under arrest for murder, Mrs. Caldwell. You have the right…"

Not listening to the Miranda rights, I only focus on finding the first bit of peace that I can. When I killed them, I felt a release, but when I killed Jimmy and thought I killed Candyce, that was out of desperation. I haven't even had the time to feel truly bad about it because I still feel it was needed in many ways. All of it was necessary.

"So he beat you? Is that why you killed him, Lisa? Him and that woman that they found on the side of the bed…is that what went on?" He lifts me from the ground with both my hands cuffed together, but instead of standing there like a puppet, I run. I don't get far because he reaches forward, yanking me back against his body.

"He hurt me," I quiver, but then end up going quiet once again. He hangs up his phone and walks us both back to what I now see as an unmarked police car, finally locating the strobe lights on the dash. Instead of sitting me in the back seat like he should, he sits me in the front, but he doesn't go around to the driver's side.

"Listen, I meant what I said to you, Lisa. I'm glad you got away from him, but the way you did it is against the law." He kneels down at my side, and when I look him in his face, the sincerity comes through. He looks around at the emptiness of the lot, and then turns back to me.

"When you came inside the store, it took a minute before I knew it was you, the same woman on the news. The photo they have of you on television isn't distraught looking and nor does it have a black eye. Honestly, you're a very nice looking lady that seemed to make a seriously bad choice behind someone making a bad choice behind your back. Do you hear me, Lisa?"

I just sit. My eyes aren't even meeting his anymore because what the hell could he possibly say to me that would make this better other than *I'm letting you go.* During our non-conversation, both gas station attendants run outside, pointing wildly like there's some YouTube brawl. The female yells, "That's the lady from the news! I knew I saw her face from somewhere when she walked in."

Congratulations, I think to myself as they behave as if I'm a super star on the next episode of an imaginary reality show called Catch That Killer. At this particular point, I'm not even ashamed. Why should I be? If anyone should be ashamed, it should be the man who gave me this damn black eye. It should be the woman who came in my house and ate my food and then laid in my bed! Who else should be ashamed besides them? Not me.

"One thing I need to confess to," I finally open my mouth. Upon taking my feet outside of the car, he stops me, but I continue, "It's okay. I'm not running. I just want to confess something that I need to confess because it's the one thing today that I did out of nothing but fear. It shouldn't have happened, but I just wasn't ready…"

He removes his arm from blocking my leg and allows me to move my feet outside the car. "What is it?"

"I killed the man that was found at my brother, Luscious Caldwell's, apartment. He was at work when I did it. As a matter of fact, I'd just picked him up at the gym and dropped him off to his new job. He's going to be a lawyer, and his car was messed up. He put his bike in the back of the trunk, and then I dropped it off for him. He didn't ask me to do it."

"You have a key?"

"Yeah. I have a key. I was leaving the apartment when Jimmy, I know him through Lug..."

"Lug?"

"Luscious, that's what I call him – Lug," I explain. "He asked me about what he'd just heard or seen on the news in a round-a-bout way, and I was in the kitchen already. When he walked up to me and tried to get me to level with him, I stabbed him in his throat." I look away from Officer Dellis, blinking away my tears. "He didn't see it coming, and I really didn't see it coming either. It all happened so fast." When my tears are under control, I look back into the eyes of the officer. "Now let my brother go. He didn't do it. Check the knife. I'm sure my prints are on it which you will have when you get me to the station."

I place my feet back into the car, and that's it. Officer Dellis is talking to me, but the person that cares really isn't me. I want to tell him to shut up, but then that might come out hostile. Then, he may just tack on another charge for absolutely nothing. While I'm sitting in the car, two cop cars come down the street, lights blaring and flashing away while I choose to stare at Smack. My whole objective is to make sure Smack gets taken care of before they take me off. I interrupt Officer Dellis who is calling my name.

"Take care of Smack."

"I already said that the dog will be taken care of for you. You haven't heard a thing I've been saying, have you?"

"No."

He's frustrated, but I can't imagine he's more frustrated than I am. He shuts the door on me while he approaches the oncoming authorities. He even locks the door. Before I can even analyze the whole situation, another officer in an official uniform starts to walk my way along with Officer Dellis who unlocks the door on his way to the car. Once at the door, a female officer takes me out of the car, frisks me – something that Officer Dellis didn't do – and then walks me over to what I find out is a very cramped back seat of a squad car. This is now my life.

Chapter 25

"Shit," he moans, having crawled across the highway to a safer spot underneath the bridge. He cradles his wound like a baby because it feels like it's going to explode. "Come on, Jack, breathe," he encourages himself as he lays his back against the concrete trying not to panic.

Cars pass by on the interstate at maximum speeds, creating hope for Jack as he tries to remain stable from the gunshot wound Candyce put on his body before shoving him out of the back seat of a car. Like his life depends on it because it really does, Jack slowly eases out as close to the highway as possible. Clearly, he doesn't want to get hit by any cars, trucks or cycles going by, but he knows he has to take a chance on getting closer to the road. There's a slight dip that, unless a jeep or truck passes by, he won't be very visible to lower riding cars. Extending his arm, he begins to wave it back and forth wildly. Several cars go by, but none stop. The last thing he wants is a passer-by to call the cops to come and get him, but if they do, he'll have to take it.

"Come on, somebody, stop. I'm dying here!" he yells, and his pleas are answered. He watches as a jeep passes by, but further on down the road, puts on the brakes to move over onto the shoulder. "Thank God." He drops his head to the ground, relieved that he doesn't have to struggle as much anymore. "That stupid bitch shot me. When I find her ass…" he complains, raising his hand again at the people he watches running toward him.

"Oh my goodness, Donald, look at him. I think he's been stabbed or shot or something!" the lady yells. "Call the ambulance because we can't put him in our car. Donald, come on!"

"I'm calling, Jenny, I'm calling! Just don't touch him, dammit. Get back. You just can't mind your business, can you?"

"Sir, are you okay? What happened?" she asks while Jack looks back at the woman's husband who is yanking her back by the arm while he tries to talk on the phone. Finally, a moaning Jack responds.

"I've been shot. Just stay back a bit like he says. I'm good. He's just trying to protect you," Jack answers her, not wanting to have any false charges of rape or anything unheard pressed against him by her husband later down the line after being admitted to the hospital. The last place he wants to go anyway is the hospital because once he gets there, the cops will come because of the gunshot wound.

"Look, sir. The ambulance is on the way, so hold tight while me and my wife get back into the car. Can you tell me what happened to you or who did this, you know, just in case something bad happens to you while we wait?"

"Donald!"

"Well, it's true, Jenny. He could die, so why not do the responsible thing and get all the information from him now?"

Jack watches as they argue over the responsible thing to do, and he is in awe at the whole thing. The very first time he tried to do one thing totally responsible by proposing to the woman he loves, she shoots him with a bullet in hopes of his death instead of a black out. Next thing he knows, he's rolling down into a big ditch with a hole in his body.

As he watches the married couple's scenario of who is right and who is wrong, he starts to giggle. About five seconds later, his giggle turns into a full out laugh, and the couple stands there in their khaki shorts and white tops with striped collars looking like they are on the way to a golf tournament. When he looks down at their shoes, he explodes into laughter because they are spotless and, to him, totally geeky.

"Donald," she stops arguing as she examines Jack's laughter. She places her hand on her chest and alerts her husband. "He's about to die! He's going hysterical!"

Jack's smile drops, and then he stutters when he fully grasps what she's saying. "What? What did you say?"

"You're going into hysteria. If the ambulance doesn't come quickly, I mean, I don't see much blood on the outside, but from the inside, you could be bleeding to death!"

"What?" Jack pushes up off the ground with his elbows. "Are you serious? This shit isn't funny. Are you freaking serious?"

"Hey watch your mouth, man. We didn't have to stop for what looks to be scum…"

"Scum? Who the hell," Jack retorts but ends up grabbing his stomach in agony. That's when he hears it. The ambulance is coming down the interstate, and what a grand entrance it's making as all the cars move onto the shoulder of the road like it's royalty. "Thank you, ma'am," Jack turns to tell the woman who is still very much concerned about him. Then he looks to her husband, gives him a mean squint and says, "I'll be sure to find you and pay you a visit to thank you personally."

Her husband takes that as a threat, so he taps his wife and they both leave the scene. The ambulance rolls to a stop ahead of Jack and in about five minutes, down the interstate rolls the stretcher while the driver slowly backs up for a better recovery position. Next thing he knows, the cops aren't far behind, and they all go to the hospital.

Chapter 26

"Did you talk to Lisa? Did you get her? She's going right up there to leave Lyndi something, so…"

"Wait a minute. Just wait, Joe, man. She's gone. I saw her up here at the cemetery. She hated me, and she loved me at the same time, but then she left. It was the last time I think I'll see her."

"You let her go, Herbert?" he asks Lisa's father.

"Yeah, I had to let her go. She killed some people, Joe. She told me herself. I just wanted her to know that I love her, but ultimately, I don't have that much influence on her life. That she let me know."

"Come on, Joe," interjects Lyndi. "Let's go. We have to go to the cemetery to get the stuff. Come on now, so we can come back up here with Lug…make sure none of these bogus cops try anything on my nephew."

Joe rushes to get off the phone because Lyndi doesn't know who he's on the phone with nor does she know that there was a meeting at the cemetery between Lisa and her long lost dad. "Okay, man, I'll see you. I have to go." He hangs up the telephone, on edge because of the secret he's hidden from his wife about Lisa and Lug's father, Herbert. "Alright, baby, let's go get it," he continues to Lyndi, hoping that everything is clear when he gets to the cemetery.

Feeling the pressure of keeping Lyndi out of jail along with Lug and Lisa, Joe tries to keep everything in perspective for her as they walk toward the exit of the hospital. Encouraging her, telling her everything from I love you to even getting her something to eat only mitigates the gravity of the situation for a short period of time. After her mind gets off of what Joe is talking about, it is overtaken again by possibly losing her niece and nephew, the only children she's been able to see as hers because of her inability to have her own. For the longest time after Linda, her twin, passed away, she began to believe that God planned for her to be there for them in place of the children she couldn't have but desperately wanted. At least, that's how she comforts herself. She never thought that things would take such a horrible turn for the worst, to possibly lose them both at the same time.

On the way down to the cemetery, Joe's nerves are shot. For the most part, he's always been a man to keep his home together, never allowing the slightest bit of trouble to disrupt the normal peace of his dwelling. Finances have always been covered, prayer life, and the overall good living that his own dad taught him to do for a healthy family, with or without his own children. Now, as he drives down the road, he feels that he's made the biggest mistake of his life. He's never hidden anything from Lyndi, ever. His stomach is in knots as he thinks about the possibility of the truth coming out about, not his lie, but his slight deception, about Herbert. When he ran into him at the gas station, he didn't go with his first inclination to tell Lyndi because he didn't want her to get involved. Now that this has happened to Lisa and Lug, guilt is circulating in his mind of what would've happened if he'd told. Maybe Lisa and Lug could have taken a different road because Herbert would have etched another path in their lives.

Lyndi's hands are constantly moving, if she isn't twiddling her thumbs, she's rubbing her knees and pulling her nails. Tears are rolling down her eyes one minute, and the next minute, her eyes are completely dried up as she stares out the car window blankly. The only thing that takes her out of her gaze is when the car hits an uneven spot on the road or if the car comes to a complete stop.

"Joe, I don't know what to do. I really don't know what to do. We don't have enough money to hire lawyers for the both of them. Both of them, Joe? What if they won't let Lug go? What if they think the whole thing is made up?"

"Lyndi, things are going to be fine. Lug is going to be fine. Lisa will, too. She may have to go to jail for some time, but she'll be fine."

"That's not fine, Joe! She won't be fine. What if this effects Lug's future as a lawyer. What if she ends up all alone? We have to die one day, Joe. Us! We have to die!"

"Enough, Lyndi! We can only do what we can with each day that comes. Now, I know you love them, but they aren't kids anymore. I love them, too, but we have to think. Just think and pray because, Lyndi," he sighs, "it's out of our hands."

He finally turns into the dark cemetery, and at first, he doesn't notice anything unusual. As he continues down the path which is incredibly hard for him to see, he approaches Linda's grave. He doesn't look to the right. Instead, he only listens as Lyndi chokes up at the sight of the grave. It's been months since she's come to her sister's side.

Joe stops the car, and Lyndi wastes no time getting out. Before she gets her feet planted firmly on the grass though, Joe reaches over and grabs her arm. His grip is so tight that it frightens her because he never yanks her in that manner.

"Wait, Lyndi."

"What?" she asks as she falls back into the car, but then she looks through the windshield in the direction that her husband is looking. There's a man in what looks like an abandoned vehicle that is parked near the woods, everything turned off.

"Wait right here?" he commands.

"Joe, no, don't go over there!"

"I'm not. Just wait." Joe gets out of the car and calls Herbert's number. Then he waits. Sure enough. The man he's staring at starts to walk toward them and speak into the phone.

"It's me, Joe," the man on the other end answers.

"Alright." Joe sits back in the seat, facing Lyndi.

"Who is that?"

"Lyndi, there's something I didn't tell you."

"What is this? Who is that, Joe, come on!" she exclaims, uncomfortable with the stalling.

"It's Herbert, baby."

"Herbert?" She leans forward, not certain about what her husband has just stated, but when she pays close attention to the man as he approaches, she suddenly looks back at her husband in shock. "Herbert? The kids' daddy?" she asks confused.

"Let me explain," Joe starts, but it's too late. Lyndi is already out of the car and charging towards Herbert like she has been waiting on this her whole life. Joe leaps from the car to catch her, and he makes it just in time as her hand reaches up in the air ready to knock Herbert in his face.

"Move, Joe!" she yells, shoving him, but not hard enough. "I'm doing your job, Herbert, and I've been doing it this whole time! Your children are grown now so what the hell do you want over here, huh?" She turns to her husband who stands in front of her. "What is all this, Joe?"

"I called him."

"Called him?" she steps back in disbelief. "You've been in contact with him all this time?"

"No, Lyndi, I ran into him at the gas station…"

Herbert interjects, "I got his number and he got mine after I told him that I'd moved back here to see my children, to finally get to know them. I…I," he stutters, "I know it's late, but I didn't know that they were in trouble, so Joe did what he thought was right to call me today and let me know about everything. I'm sorry, Lyndi."

"Moved back? Why didn't you tell me, Joe?" she asks her husband confused on why he would take the side of a man who abandoned her sister and children.

"He told me he moved back in the area, but he wanted to get things more situated and figure out how to approach Lisa and Lug. It made sense to me as a man…"

"No it doesn't!" she disagrees. "Oh hell no it doesn't." Then, her attention goes back to Herbert. "You are their father! You approach them as such, but after that long, Herbert, you really should have never come because you're too damn late."

"Stop it, Lyndi," Joe orders.

"And you let go of me, Joe!" She glares back at Herbert and warns, "You stay away from Lisa and Lug. They're gonna make it without you." She turns to go to Linda's grave to get the money but stops when Herbert responds.

"It's too late, Lyndi. I met Lisa here. She told me everything she did, and she even cussed me out. In the end though, she still loves me…and I love her, her and Lug. I'm going to finish paying for his education, Lyndi. I know that's not much, but I've saved a load of money up," he says reaching in his pocket. Then he pulls a pen out of what looks to be a checkbook. "I can write the check out now for whatever it is…"

"Save that money! Keep it!" She spits on the ground and keeps walking toward the money that Lisa says she left at the grave, but Joe nods at Herbert, resulting in him writing the check out to his son in the amount of fifteen thousand dollars. "I'll write the rest out when I transfer it. Thank you, Joe."

"Yeah," he says quietly, taking the check and quickly putting it in his wallet. "I'll be sure it gets put to use."

"When you left Lug at the hospital, how was he? Can I go see him?"

"They're not letting anyone back there. They think he committed murder…"

"Lisa said…"

"I know…I know," he groans. "Thing is, confessing to us doesn't set Lug free. The cops need to hear it, and then, only hopefully, they let him loose. Until then we have to wait. He's healing from the gunshot wound though."

"Come, Joe, let's go. Got no time for this, and over my sister's grave? I won't let you come and do worse than what you did then!" She stomps off to the door of the car. "You can just leave, didn't even come and pay damn respect to my sister when she passed away," she hollers, not yet satisfied with not being able to fight him, so she drops the money back on the ground and charges him again.

"No, Joe, let her come," he states as he moves away from Joe who is attempting to block the oncoming assault. Joe then retreats, allowing Lyndi to go insane on his face.

She slaps him over and over again, and Herbert stands there and takes it. His face welcomes an onslaught of rage from his ex-sister-in-law, and he feels like he deserves every bit of it. After slapping him enough, she balls up her fist, but then Herbert finally reaches up and grabs her by the wrist. Joe intervenes and then Herbert lets her wrist go.

"Why did you do that to my sister? She loved you, Herbert, and I swear if you'd never walked out on her," she pants to catch her breath, "she would be here with us today. That was my sister!"

"I'm sorry. I am, Lyndi, but I can't change…"

"You damn right you can't." That's it for Lyndi. She walks away, picks up the money from the ground, and gets into the car. Joe walks back as well as Herbert just stands there with his sore face and nowhere to go but home.

Chapter 27

"Ahhh! Ouch!" yells Jack as they get him onto the surgery table. "What the hell is that pain?" he complains as they turn him over.

"Whoever shot you didn't know what they were doing or you got extremely lucky because there isn't an exit wound, but there is also no internal bleeding," proclaims the doctor who is already robed down. "Your bullet we're going to leave intact as a part of your body. Too risky to remove it because, frankly, you may bleed to death right here on this table. We don't want that. It looks like you are going to be okay based on the scans, so all we need to do now is patch you up and then you'll be all ready to begin the healing process. Nurse," he calls pointing down at an area of his body.

"Are you serious?" he laughs. "Seriously? Oh man, doc, thanks! Ouch!"

"Give him a little bit more...for the pain, and we're going to do a topical also for this hole in the front." The doctor addresses Jack again. "You're going to be just fine...in more pain later but fine."

As the doctor explains to Jack exactly what will happen within the next thirty minutes to days, he's not even listening. The only thing he can think about is getting back at Candyce for trying to kill him. Every muscle in his body, including the shot ones, are grateful to be alive just to exact revenge on the woman he thought had love for him. The more he thinks about Candyce getting away with attempted murder, the more he wants to jump from the table, go find a gun and blast her, but he can't. This is why he's about to boil over, especially now that he knows he's about to leave the hospital in at the minimum of two weeks.

He elects to watch as the doctor goes forth with the patching of his broken and wounded body, but even though his eyes are glued on what's going on just a couple body parts down via a mirror, his mind is still on vengeance. How he is going to love showing up at Candyce's house to bash her head through the wall before turning her in to the cops. He remembers how he risked his own life and freedom to get an engagement ring that he knew she would love, that he even thought she was worth, until she shot him down like a dog. Jack balls up his fists while the doctor patches him up and slams it down onto the bed rail. The doctor and nurse jump, but Jack doesn't flinch. His face is beet red, and his breathing is erratic.

"Sir, are you okay, sir?" the nurse asks, checking over every machine hooked to him that shows his heart rate and more.

Jack simply looks at her and nods. His teeth grind and his eyes seem to sink back into his head with each breath he takes through his nostrils.

"Sir?"

"I'm fine. Just angry that someone shot me and left me for dead. It was someone who was supposed to love me. Can you believe that?" he asks in a massive attempt to keep foul language from his mouth.

"Okay, sir. I'm sorry, but you're here now. Try to relax as the doctor is taking care of the situation. The cops will be in to question you about the accident."

"Accident? Hell, the shit was purposeful. Like hell it was an accident. Wait, I'm sorry…just angry."

"Understood there, Jack," the doctor chimes in. "I would be too there if someone put a bullet in me, especially if it was someone that I know."

"It was my fuckin' fiancée! No, fuck that. It was the girl I was dating that took my ring, shot *my* ass, and then ran off with the most expensive thing I ever owned in my whole damn life. As a matter of fact, look in my damn wallet. Get it. Put her ass on blast. Give that to the cops for me. Are they here? Give it to them just in case some unlucky shit happens to me on this table because that's the woman, the only picture you will find in there besides my driver's license, that shot me. I put that on my life!"

Jack feels a deep weight lift from his shoulders when he releases the information to the nurse and doctor. He even watches as the nurse goes ahead and gets the photo out of Candyce, handing it to another associate as she comes back to work with the doctor. He can finally calm down now as he waits to be sealed all up and moved to his room so that he can get some rest the happy way.

**

"We just need to get a statement from you, Mr. Jack Seedman, about the events that led up to your shooting, and if this photo is in fact the photo of the woman who shot you," the detective asks as Jack lies back on a pillow while the television plays directly in front of him, elevated on the wall. Jack presses mute so that he can give the detective his full attention.

"Yes, sir. That woman, my ex, just shot me in the back of the car for absolutely nothing and dumped my ass out of the car right after she did it. Hell, I must have passed out or something from the shot because I woke up at the bottom of a hill, like a ditch. We were coming down, or no…getting off onto the highway, and I can't even really tell you where I was, but when her friend turned onto a ramp, Candyce shot me! I don't even know why!" he shouts, lifting his hands to his sides. "I thought we were gonna get married and all, but that shit is full of shit."

"So someone was driving her?"

"Yes. We were riding with her best friend in the whole entire universe," he says sarcastically and rolling his eyes in disgust, "named Lisa. I don't know what the hell, but she's the one that picked us up from the airport. Next thing you know, Candyce shoots me, and that's the end of the story! I think she killed me to get away with the ring, to be honest," he states, but then realizing a little too late what he just told the officer, he quiets down.

"The ring?"

"Just a little ring I bought her, you know, a commitment ring. It wasn't the most expensive thing, but worth enough." Jack's heart rate escalates as he thinks about how many ways the words that he let slip in his own dumb anger could get him many years in prison if they find Candyce and the ring. It was obvious for him not to discuss the drug trafficking, but for some reason unknown to himself, he didn't put the same weight on the jewelry heist versus the drugs. As he continues to think about it, the scenario of Candyce ratting his robbery out to the cops as revenge on him for turning her in makes him clam up.

"Where can I find Candyce…her address, last name, in detail …as much information as you can give us… as well as the Lisa lady."

Jack just sits there staring at the man who may not only end up arresting Candyce but him as well. His throat gets drier than what it already is, and then he abruptly asks for some water. "Nurse," he calls from the button on his bed. "Will you please bring some water. I'm fresh out and thirsty." The nurse answers back positively, and Jack fixes his thin robe and adjusts his cover and the tilt of his bed. Then, the cop asks again.

"Mr. Seedman," the detective sighs as if he's having a long day, "I've been through this many times, and I can tell you've just gotten hesitant about the matter. You have to understand that telling us is helping yourself. Obviously, this woman didn't love you, and if what you're saying is true, she needs to be arrested. It's not even up to you to press charges. This is now in my territory, so don't hinder your own justice. Last name of your ex, please?

"Candyce Moore," Jack finally cooperates. "She's one of the pretty descendants of the Moore family."

"The Moore family?"

"Yeah, that's the one."

"Breaking news," alerts the television loudly, so Jack turns it down a tad and continues to listen. "Earlier today, police were on a search for one Lisa Caldwell who was wanted for questioning in the case of a double murder at her home. Now, police have arrested her, and it seems there is another murder that has taken place by the hands of this woman whom is being described as a danger to the community as a whole. There will be more on the next news update."

"Oh shit."

The detective observes Jacks demeanor, and then asks him the most loaded question that he can ask based off of the information that Jack voluntarily provided. "Is this the Lisa who was driving the vehicle when you were shot, Mr. Seedman?"

Jack immediately jumps out of his skin and turns to the detective like it's his first time seeing him. Then, he stares back at the television. "Murder? I had nothing to do with that shit! Murder? I don't even kill flies, detective, I swear I don't. I swat 'em, that's it, and those little assholes just keep on buzzin'."

"Is this woman, Lisa Caldwell, your ex's best friend?"

"Yeah, yeah, that's her. Killed three people? When did this happen? I just got in from Jamaica. The airlines can prove it," he tenses up in full defense of himself at the magnitude of charges that he thinks could hit him at any moment.

"Jack, I'm here to find Candyce, your shooter. Now, do you think that Lisa and Candyce set up your shooting? What are the events that led up to your..."

"I told you! She picked us up from the airport, Lisa did, and was taking us home. We went riding around first, but other than that...the riding around was because Candyce wanted to look for another house. I proposed to her, but then she shot me. Like what the hell?" he exclaims, tossing his hands into the air. "Did I think Lisa and Candyce set me up? No, I don't think so. Lisa's not that type..."

"Isn't she?" he asks a baffled Jack. "You say Candyce shot you, so you really don't think she *and* Lisa could set you up?"

Jack thinks about his question. Everything may not have been what it seemed to him as he remembers all the way back to Jamaica. Whenever Candyce acted shyly, was she really being secretive? When she laughed, was it really to throw him off? Or how about when she just insisted that Lisa come to pick them up from the airport instead of a cab? Another thing, did Candyce know about the murders and did she help Lisa before they left?"

"When did these murders happen and where?"

"Sometime between last night and the early morning we suppose. Were you in Jamaica then?"

"Yes, I guess I was…both me and Candyce were. Shit, this doesn't make sense!" Jack thinks back to when they were going back to Candyce's house and saw a load of officers there. They turned around and fled, and Candyce was just as confused as he was.

Jack sits up in the bed but continues to look down as the detective uses his cell phone and walks toward the hospital room door. He listens hard as he tells another officer to question Lisa repeatedly about her story because he has another potential key witness to a deeper story than what they know so far. The palms of his hands are sweating so he quickly puts them underneath the white sheet and wipes them off. The nurse comes into the room.

"Here is your water, Mr. Seedman. Are you doing alright? While I'm in here, let me just take your vitals," she states as she begins her duties of reflex testing and pulse taking.

"Nurse," he whispers.

"Yes?"

"Am I going to be arrested? Like are there cops outside my door?"

"No," she responds uneasily. When she's done, she walks back out of the room.

"Well, Mr. Seedman," the officer sits back down, slouching on the chair. "It looks like I'll be here for a minute or two. This may be your lucky day, depending on how Lisa answers these questions. We may just find your shooter."

The back of Jack's head hits the pillow, and he shuts his eyes in the middle of the officer's slick smile.

Chapter 28

Pulling up a chair and sitting on it backwards across the table from me is a female cop, a brunette with newly waxed eyebrows and her hair in a ponytail. She's not even looking at me but at a couple of pages of paperwork in front of her. If my hands were free of these cuffs, I would go for it, but then, I wouldn't get too far because I have on this jail house outfit that, mixed with my black and red eye, won't get me beyond the officers outside the door.

This room doesn't bring the same feeling that I get when I'm looking at the movies. Maybe it's because I'm the one sitting inside it now, the main character of my own flick, but things aren't going my way. I was supposed to…

"So, Mrs. Lisa Caldwell, I'm Officer Thomas. I'm going to cut to the chase because it's late, and you have a lot to tell me. Why don't you get started?"

Is she kidding me? Is that the way you ask anyone for information and really expect them to give it to you straight? "I need a lawyer," I respond. I feel like since they know everything about me, they should be telling me my story, the story of my whole life.

"Listen, Lisa, the story that you already gave is that you killed a person already. We have the confession, but now we have a recorder that we would like for you to put your voice on. We really don't need it to have you charged with murder due to you earlier confession. Do you understand? Now, if you would, I would like to get out of here before day break because you've really worked us today, all day and night," she says frustrated with me. I could care less though. As I sit here as still as a board, staring back into the eyes of my enemy, I begin to

221

understand that she just wants more pieces of her throne, a possible pat on the back for breaking me down, or maybe this could be her first interrogation. Hell, it's my first time being interrogated. Therefore, instead of fighting it, she's right. I already confessed, so I'll give her the blow by blow, every single detail.

She appears surprised when I begin. "We got in a fight, and I ended up the punching bag. Robert, my husband, hit me, and after he chased me from the house," I pause, "I got into the car and left. I went to a motel for a little bit, some hours, but decided to go back to the house later, around, I think, two o'clock in the morning maybe. Now, before our fight, I'd made the perfect candlelit dinner," I express with a smile on my face. "I can smell it now. It was a full course meal, and I'd slaved over that meal just for him, but when he got home, he found something." I look to the floor as I recall what Robert did. "He found something, as he usually did, to get angry about. His thing to be angry at was me," I reveal, staring back into the officer's eyes while she slowly gets blurrier as a result of my eyes filling with tears.

"Yeah, he uh…was angry at me, and I didn't know why. I hadn't known why for months and months. My whole thing was that it would pass, you know. I just kept looking my best and smiling, taking less for me and putting in more for him, just to make his days easier. Anyway…" I clear my throat. "When I got back home to try and smooth things over with him, despite the fact that he'd hit me in my face, I notice my food eaten. Yeah," I nod my head. "As soon as I walk through the door, the candlelight was melted down, and the food, on both plates, was eaten."

"I went to the kitchen and got a knife. I remember doing it, you know, because obviously, an intruder was in my house."

"Doing what?"

"Getting the knife. I knew I was going to need it because I saw her clothes off in my house. It was first her shirt and then his. One was on top of the other, and then I followed the trail of the bra and underwear down my hallway. From the hall, I saw them lying in my bed and on my sheets," I continue, struggling not to become enraged again. "They didn't even hear me," I laugh. "That's what was so funny about it because I live there, you know, and Robert didn't think twice about me possibly coming back home before he brought his whore inside my bed, underneath my sheets. God knows she probably would have lived if she wasn't in my bed, but...she was and she knew it." I can feel my face turning to stone as I say what happens next. "So I slit her fucking throat."

"Robert," I adjust myself the best I can in the small chair and take a deep breath. "He looks up at me from the bed in disbelief because I was leaning over him when I slit her neck from one side to the other as hard as I could. My husband... mine... looked shocked that *I* was so upset that I guess he got scared and got up. I stabbed him though, so I guess he was the one that got fucked for real. Me and my black ass eye stabbed the hell out of his ass while his beast of a girlfriend...I heard her sucking for air, gasping. She already messed my sheets up, so she owed me anyway and paid with her life," I shrug. "Robert, though, he was struggling, so I stabbed him again until he fell on the floor. I watched as he crawled up the hallway, all the way to the kitchen where he died. I stabbed him three times."

"Three times?" the officer repeats.

I lean over into the microphone of the recorder and repeat, "Three times."

"Lisa Caldwell, let's take a break because you say you stabbed him three times, but that can't be right."

"And why can't it be right? I was there. I know."

"Your husband had forty stab wounds, Lisa." Then, she pulls out a couple of pictures from a folder. "Here are some photos of what is left of your husband."

I don't hesitate to glance through them. As she moves each photo slowly, I see his mutilated body, however, I know I didn't do that. I only stabbed him three times, each time I even felt the force coming from my arm to his body. Even when the knife came out, I remember how it looked.

"That's something that I didn't do," I respond, staring up into her face. "So you can stop with the photos."

"Lisa, people saw you shopping…"

"Yeah, I went shopping as soon as the store opened up. I was caring for my best friend's dog, Smack. She's a rotten pooch, and she wouldn't eat her food. Can't let the dog die, right? I went and got her something."

"I was getting ready to say that people in the store alerted the authorities because you were covered in blood. Do you really think that three stab wounds would have your body covered in blood?"

Still sitting motionless, replaying the events of Robert's death over and over again, I can only remember stabbing him three times. "Depending on where I stab, yes, but I didn't hit an artery because…"

"Mrs. Caldwell, there's a camera shot of you at the grocery store, walking inside and walking back out. Each time, you were covered in blood. People stopped to look…did you not see that because we saw it on the surveillance?"

For a second, I become startled by what the officer is saying, but then I remember all those people at the store, how I thought they were gawking at my black eye, and how they shielded their children from me as I walked by. "Forty times…" I state. "I don't remember that much. I know I stabbed him three…"

"Either way, you wanted to kill him."

I stare back at the officer with the utmost seriousness. "Yes." My voice doesn't shake nor do I. "It was self-defense." That's when my tears begin to fall as I stare back at a woman who looks like she has it all together. Although pretty, she has a face of stone, almost like she can't understand what Robert put me through. I used to be in that same dream land right along with her, so I explain. "You sit there looking at me as if you never had your heart broken. If someone came up to you and shattered your body with a bat, those are the bruises you can see. You can see all the bruises and all the bumps, just like with this," I state, pointing to my black eye. "But what about the bruising and the scarring that someone does to you when they assault you to the fucking core, huh?" She doesn't answer, so I shout at my loudest, "What about when they fucking tear your heart apart! Does that not hurt? Is that not somebody trying to kill you, abusing you…destroying your very soul?" my voice quivers. Then, I wipe the tear from my eye with the tip of my shoulder. "Yeah it is. It's assault and battery with intent to kill, dammit, because none of you mother fuckers in here can visibly see what he did to me on the inside!" I go quiet and look away at the walls. "And that's pretty fucked up if you ask me. It's that visible shit that counts in the court of law. Only God knows my pain."

For the first time, when I place the officer back into my line of vision, she isn't looking back at me. Instead, she appears a bit uneasy, and it's there when I know that she isn't as tough as her demeanor assumes. Her heart has been where mine is now, except she didn't follow through.

"You've been there, haven't you?"

She doesn't answer me, but instead takes a deep breath and continues on, defying what I've already figured out. She's been where I've been, and she knows what I feel. The problem is that she's still living in the damn denial that she's totally over it when fact is, she's just learned to live with it. I ignore her and continue my story, almost for her sake, leaning my body closer to the table, so much so that my chest is right up against the edge.

"Forty times or three, I stabbed him to death, and I got my life back. I felt like all he took from me, I got back, and like you said, I went to the grocery store when day broke to get Smack some food. Then I left to go take my brother to work at his new internship job at a law firm. His car broke down."

"Your brother's name?"

"Lug." I sit back in the chair, more relaxed now that I'm talking about the best part of the day. I love seeing my brother. "His real name is Luscious. Anyway, he called me, and I picked him up. He loaded his bike...that's what he was riding...in the trunk of the car, and then, I took him to work. After I dropped him off, I didn't tell him that I was going to go to his apartment to put his bike back inside. I have a key. I didn't mean any harm, but when I got inside, a friend of his stopped by before I was able to leave named Jimmy. I'd left the door open, and when he came in, he mildly provoked me, too. Maybe he didn't see

226

it as that, but now that I look back on it, he asked me about what you guys put on the news about me. To me, I was cornered, so even though he was always a nice guy, I had to cut his throat to keep living my life. Lug never even knew. I just locked up his apartment," I sighed, "And left."

"Is that all?"

"That's all I'm talking about unless you want me to talk about when I brushed my teeth, combed my hair or went to the toilet in all this mayhem."

She clears her throat, and begins to speak again. "A slick tongue isn't going to get you far, Mrs. Caldwell, because we have a witness that says that you were going to pick up some friends from the airport. Did you ever make it?"

"Yeah, I did."

"Well?"

"They were just getting in from Jamaica. I went to get them and dropped them off where they needed to go," I quickly reveal, but right after that, my mind returns to how Nate and his goons thought it funny to wet me up. Even funnier to him how he thought it would be to command my murder through my own best friend. Therefore, since no one knows I tried to kill Candcye, I continue. "I took them to a guy name Nate. That's how I found out that she trafficked drugs into the country with her man named Jack. Come to find out though that Jack wasn't really her man. It was Nate. I can't tell you how to get back to the house, but you'll find dope there if you ever stop worrying about me." She doesn't laugh at my sarcastic joke, so I continue with the story.

"Went there, and when we got back on the road, she shot Jack to death. You should find his body on the side of the highway somewhere...if you look hard enough and if Nate hasn't already gotten rid of the body. Candyce blew him to bits as I got off on the ramp." I think about holding back on the story, but what the hell? They're both dead. They can't serve time, and fuck Nate. "By the way, Nate told her to kill me, too, but I got away from her before she got the chance to do it." I already have three counts of murder headed my way, why go with a fourth charge of dumping a dead body that I didn't even kill? They can find Nate for that. Sucker. Who's gonna get wet now? They'll never find her body and that expensive ass ring Jack took though. Oh yeah...the ring.

"By the way, right before Candyce shot her flunky fiancé, like a couple hours before, he proposed to her with a huge ring. Are there any jewelry stores missing a big ass ring, officer, like from a heist?" I ask.

She stares at me as if this whole thing is a waste of her time. Honestly, if it is, she should let me go. All I did was get a bunch of assholes off the streets because her lazy ass won't get up and do it herself. She's so stiff. I don't like her at all.

"Hello?" I speak loudly. "I just asked you a question? Are any stores missing a big ass ring?"

"There are always robberies, Mrs. Caldwell."

"This ring isn't chump change. Up state, do you recall that big heist?"

"You mean in Orlando?"

"Yep. That's Jack. I guess he got his due, huh?"

The officer finally breaks and smiles. It's the first smile that I've gotten out of her since the whole interrogation started. I mean, I know I appear like a hard core killer, but throughout the day, I started to accept my fate as the nice, trusting and loving lady that I am. I just don't take shit anymore is all.

"Well, where is this Candyce?"

"Shouldn't you know?" At my question, she seems confused. "Weren't you all at her home today?" I ask, toying with her a while since this is the last bit of great conversation that I might get in a long while.

"I'm not here to answer your questions..."

"Well, this is a waste then." I lean forward once again with a horrible attitude because I know I have nothing to lose. Then, I spitefully and quietly say, "Find her yourself."

She grabs the tape recorder and heads out of the room which leaves me alone. I sit and think someone is supposed to come and get me, but they never do. For now I'm just sitting with nowhere to go, so I start to roll my head back and forth on the edge of the table and wait...that is until I begin to concentrate on the pointed corners of the table. As I roll my head back and forth, I count the years I could get sentenced with each roll. Life in prison is what I'm going to be awarded for my sins. I could feel it in my spirit, therefore, I stop rolling my head on the table. As I keep it stagnant and leaning, I begin to pray.

"Jesus, I already know that you know what I did. You know while mom was here, she raised me better. You also know that I know better. Being that I don't know how to feel sorry for killing Robert and his girlfriend, I do feel bad about Jimmy and Candyce. I want to repent about," I choke up in the middle of my prayer, "my actions and feelings where they are wrong. I don't know how to let go of my anger, Lord, but I know that I need your forgiveness for it all is why I'm asking. Please forgive me for those murders and all the bad I've done in my life. Please take care of Lug and forgive him, my aunt and uncle, as well as my dad, and please forgive me for what I'm about to do now."

It takes only two hard jumps on the chair to move it to the sharp edge of the table. I figure that I'm on camera, so I don't waste anymore time. "Please forgive me, Lord, for everything including myself. I can't live in prison, and I have to choose," I continue with one tear coming from my eye, "how I must die."

I quickly lean my body as far away from the edge of the table that I can, and then I aim for my temple. I swing my head as hard as I can with visions of my brother succeeding in law school, and my temple hits.

Chapter 29

"Well, I have some great news, Jack!" the officer exclaims, popping up from the chair after hanging up the phone with another officer. "Lisa was just interrogated, my fine sir, and you were telling the truth. Candyce did shoot the hell out of you. There are two or three problems though."

Jack's heart feels like it's going to explode. Sweat pours from his head, and his hair melts onto his scalp like he just stepped out of the shower. The smell from his underarms reeks as he has been lying there with his eyes shut for the entire time while panic ripped through his body up until the officer's phone rang.

"What problems, officer?"

"The first problem is that we don't know where Candyce is. The second is that you were in the middle of trafficking drugs from Jamaica to this wonderful coast we have here. Were you not?"

Jack doesn't say one word. The epiglottis in his throat continues to try and swallow moist spit, but instead, it gulps dry, nauseating air. The officer notices and gives him another fresh, white paper cup full of ice cold water from the pitcher. Then, he continues.

"Silence is a virtue, son, but you chose to remain silent at the wrong time. You see, Lisa, already said that she took you to a guy named Nate's house. That's where some of that money came from in the car Lisa was caught in, from a drug deal. Thing is, not only is there a drug trafficking problem, but there's the ring thing. Were you involved in that robbery up in Orlando? No need to lie because we can fiddle with the surveillance tapes if need be." He walks closer to the bed. "Lisa said your fiancée shot you after you proposed and didn't even give you that ring back when she pushed you out of that car, did she, Jack?"

Jack's chest begins to swell up and down like he's hyperventilating. He starts to get up from the bed in the most superior effort he can give to get away from what he considers as the end of his life, but the officer thwarts his efforts by impeding his way. Jack then falls back atop the bed in pain and sorrow, his eyes searching the room for another way out. The only other way is through the window, and he can't bust through it.

"You should have shot your girl Lisa a memo that you aren't dead after all. Maybe she wouldn't have spilled the beans. Jack Seedman, you're about to be under arrest for a jewelry heist, son. Just as soon as they finish watching the surveillance tapes and matching the guys on the tape with your face, that's a wrap. Technology is pretty good these days, son. It's just a phone call away. And then when we find this Candyce lady of yours with that big, nice ring," the officer smiles, "that drug trafficking thing will be solid as solid can get. That'll be two witnesses to the trafficking charge, Jack, and who knows how much evidence she has on her?" He pulls out his cuffs and swings them around and around. Jack lies back on the bed, staring at the white, empty wall in front of him. Praying for a miracle, but it doesn't come. One hour later, Jack is arrested for taking part in one of the biggest jewelry heists the city of Orlando has ever seen. His last words before being read his rights on the hospital bed are...

"I'm sorry." Then he cries inside the room all alone, allowing his own thoughts about prison to terrify him while he clings onto the hope that they don't find

Candyce who can seal his fate, if she squeals, with another charge – trafficking drugs.

Chapter 30

"What are you doing? Sir, what are you doing?" Lyndi asks as she chases behind officers on the way to Lug's hospital room. Joe stops her, and she immediately calms down, having now realized that there is nothing that she can do about it. Lyndi doesn't want to make things worse so she waits with Joe down the hallway.

She watches the officers enter Lug's room while the officer that sits on the chair outside of the room stands up.

"Joe, what do you think is going on?"

"I don't know, baby. We should just keep praying is all."

"Lisa's not picking up her phone...I just don't know, Joe!" she exclaims. "Did she pick up for you at all?"

"No, nothing. Let's let our concern right now be for Lug since she already confessed to the murders." He holds his hand up. "Now, Lyndi, don't say one word. You have to be able to take this. Lisa's going to prison. She knows it, and I know it. It's high time you accept it, too. It hurts, but if someone killed her, wouldn't you want justice?"

Lyndi doesn't respond. She only stares back at her husband like she's never met him before a day in her life. Her lip shakes, but then she finally comes to grips with what he is saying and has been trying to get her to do since everything went down. Then, another officer comes down the hallway. He's coming directly toward them when he stops.

"Will you step over here with me, please, sir...ma'am?"

"Yes sir," Joe responds as he takes Lyndi confidently by the hand and forces her to follow. She doesn't say one word. All she does is look down at the floor trying to maintain her composure.

They all walk into the same private room provided to them earlier, and they all sit down. The officer turns down his cell phone, unbuttons his jacket, and leans forward preparing to speak to Joe and Lyndi.

"As you know, we have been on a hard and diligent search for your niece, Lisa. We got her in custody, and she went willingly with no problems. She was very uh... cooperative... with police and the interrogation at the police station, giving a full confession to authorities." He clears his throat and adjusts his seated position which makes Lyndi and Joe uneasy. The officer continues, "I received a call," he pauses as another officer enters the room. "I just got word that Lisa has attempted to commit suicide inside the interrogation room. Right now, she is unresponsive...I'm so sorry..."

"Oh God, oh my sweet Lord Jesus, help me," Lyndi whispers quietly as her body slides from the seat and falls to the floor. "No!" she screams so loudly that it seems inconsolable. "No, God, no don't let it be, Jesus, no...oh God. No, Jesus, no! Noo!"

Joe falls to the floor to hold her, but once he feels the weight of her inner pain, he breaks his strong demeanor and ends up crying as well. The officers simply remain inside the room until Joe asks them how she tried to commit suicide.

"Sir, the officer left the interrogation room to discuss with others the recorded confession for only a couple of minutes. Apparently, your niece, who was handcuffed at the time, moved herself over to the edge of the table and flung the side of her head against the point, causing injury through her temple to her brain. If not brain damage, she could have hit her head so hard that…" In the middle of his statement, a nurse enters the door, notifying him of the arrival of the prisoner Lisa Caldwell.

"Lisa! My baby, Lisa," Lyndi breathlessly calls as she lifts herself from the floor. Joe grabs her by the waist, and the officers leave the room. Joe and Lyndi try to follow behind but are stopped by the nurse and officer who instruct them to stay behind because they won't be allowed to see her anyway until doctors try to stabilize her.

"So she's not dead, Joe! She's not dead, baby! Oh, Jesus, please hear my plea, Lord. Please, have mercy on her, Jesus. Please! Lord, what she did was wrong, but please forgive us. Please, have mercy and heal her." Lyndi continues to pray as Joe prays along with her which they both know is the best thing to do, for not only their niece, but for the families that she has effected by her cold blooded sins.

There's a knock on the door, and then it opens, interrupting their prayers. It's the liaison. "You may now see your nephew Luscious. He's been set free. I'll take you on back. I'm so sorry…"

"You didn't do one thing but help us through this time. You've been kind. Thank you," Joe states. He then looks at Lyndi who is still out of it. "He's free now, baby. Come on." Even though the news is great, it's hard to celebrate when Lisa is near or at her death.

"Follow me then," the liason responds with a concerned appearance. "I've prepared the room for you with two recliners, and if you need anything at all, let me know. There's fruit juice sandwiches and water in the room as well as wash cloths and toothbrushes being that you've been here for so long." Her heels click against the floor as she quickly walks toward Luscious' room, Lyndi and Joe enter, and the liaison leaves, closing the door behind her.

"Aunt Lyndi!" he cries.

"Hi, baby, oh don't cry now, don't cry," Lyndi responds, attempting to conceal the fact that Lisa is struggling for her life. Joe goes to the other side of the bed while Lyndi places both her arms around Lug as they embrace. While he hugs his aunt, Lug holds his hand into a fist for his uncle to give him a fist bump. Joe does, and just as soon as their fists part, someone else comes through the door – a person that neither one of them expect.

The man walks inside, and removes his cap from his head. It's Herbert, Lug's father, and when Lug looks toward the door, he recognizes everything about him because he has actually kept a picture of him inside his wallet ever since he owned one. Before his Aunt Lyndi moves away from him, he speaks.

"Dad?"

Lyndi quickly releases Lug and turns around. Her blood boils, but Joe looks at her sternly. She then turns back to look into Lug's face, and in his face, she sees a slight hint of happiness. That's when she glares at Herbert and storms out of the room while Herbert ignores her, keeping his eyes on the son he hasn't seen for years. Joe eases his way out of the room.

Herbert walks over to his son, and unlike Lisa, Lug reaches out as far as he can. When Herbert sees his son is willing to reach out to him, he moves quickly to show his

237

love right back to him. When they embrace, it's so tight until Lug has to tap his father, and he backs up only a little so that he can see his son's face up close.

"I was here, Lug. I promise I was. I'd spoken to your Uncle Joe weeks ago, but he promised me that he would let me come to see you on my own time. I'm sorry. I didn't know this would happen because I heard things were going so good for you both that I didn't want to mess it up."

"You wouldn't have messed it up, dad," he cries. "You wouldn't have messed up. You would have just made everything just that much better." He wipes his eyes. "I got shot, and Lisa is in trouble. The cops set me free because she…"

"I already know. You're not by yourself though. You won't be anymore. I saw your sister before they got her. She told me everything."

"Dad, I'm sorry. I tried to help her as much as I could but it backfired, and I got shot…"

"Shhhh! Shut up!" He covers Lug's mouth. "What you just said will make them think that you were in on killing that man. Never speak another word about helping anybody, do you understand?" He removes his hand from his son's mouth. "Her wish to me is that you finish school, and you will. I wasn't going to come up, but I couldn't help it. You're my son, and I'll kill myself to help you pay whatever it is you need to pay. Your uncle, he has the fifteen thousand dollar check just for you. I'll be writing more. Don't incriminate yourself. Your sister, she knows how much you love her. That would break her heart."

At that, Lug goes quiet, taking heed to the father whom hasn't been in his life to give him instruction on anything as a grown man. Instead of talking about Lisa while also being oblivious of her being near death, he shows his dad the gunshot wound.

"It entered here and went out. It was a miracle of God that I'm here right now. They robbed me," he says, not mentioning the thievery he did to others on their credit cards. He thinks that somehow karma came back to get him, but God is giving him a second chance. Therefore, he listens to his dad and keeps quiet about the robber he beat down in the car in self defense.

"Well, God is good, Lug, and I can't thank him enough." He stares at his son like he needs to ask him something, but nothing comes out. Lug feels the tension.

"Dad, we all have to start over some time. I'm finding that out the hardest way ever, and you should be finding that out right now, too. It's good to meet you again."

"Thanks, son," he responds, but then backs away. "Let me get out of here so I can go and talk to Joe for a minute. Let your aunt come back inside."

Lug nods, and he watches his dad leave. As soon as he walks out the door, Lyndi walks in slowly with tears in her eyes. "Lug, I have something to tell you about your sister. She's fighting for her life."

Chapter 31

"You can go on break for about five minutes. There's the television, radio and even a remote, just don't turn it up too loud. Everybody who doesn't already know, this is Raigen, the new third shift nurse who is on her first day on the unit, but she's definitely not new to the field. She has at least five years behind her," states the head nurse, "and she's well qualified." She looks back at Raigen. "I need you to stand on watch for the two bed room. One they have stable enough now, but on a breathing machine. Tried to commit suicide. The other will be moved today. Are you comfortable while I meet with the staff in the hallway about a problem area or do you need…"

"No ma'am. I've done this many times. Thanks."

"Good. Just go pop a snack in your mouth, use the bathroom, and I'll send you on a ten when I'm done. We're short-handed tonight, so I'm glad you're on board."

As soon as the head nurse walks away, Raigen whips out her cell phone and calls her man whom she hasn't spoken to since earlier in the day – Jimmy. She takes a seat, trying to remain calm, but her gut is uneasy. Although she's pregnant, she knows the bad feeling she's having isn't due to the pregnancy. That's when her ears tune in to what the ladies around her are talking about.

"Girl, who knew she would end up right here of all places." The nurse then lessens the sound of her voice to a whisper. "Her name is Lisa Caldwell…that's the girl who killed her own husband today!"

Raigen freezes at the name and hangs up her cell phone.

"Stop!"

"No! I knew her from school, and she was never some psycho. Always very nice, and as a matter of fact, me and her hung out at times. I can't imagine her killing her man...well, yes, I can if that woman he was with was his girlfriend. Damn, that."

"But wait, did you know she even confessed to another murder? Y'all, don't say shit, but..." Another nurse leans in toward each woman. "My cousin was one of the cops out there, and word is, she slit some dude name James throat in her brother's house."

"The guy that's on the other floor? That brother?"

"Not lying. Swear on my pink-i-toe. Don't say shit because I don't want my ass fired, but yeah...let's go." Then the woman speaking looks at Raigen. "That's a solid crazy heifer in that room, so don't turn your back, jack, half dead or not." Then she addresses everyone else. "Let's get this over with. Come on."

"What was his last name...the James you were talking about?" Raigen asks holding back her tears from the ladies as she pretends to re-tighten her sneaker. Her fingers begin to shake, so she stops.

"Uhmmm...Madison. Madison...that's his name. James Madison." She walks away. "I got the scoop, y'all!"

Raigen simply gets up and walks past the other ladies, making it to the bathroom without uttering a word. Although no words form from her lips, when she hears no one in the room, she drops to the tiled floor and weeps. She remembers where Jimmy told her he was going while she slept on their bed, and it was to Lug's apartment. Her eyes move left to right along with her hands trying to feel for some type of comfort as she hears over and over again Lug tell her that he just got home.

She suddenly falls silent and stands to her feet, her hand on her womb. The sink is directly in front of her, and she moves toward it to clean off her face. She's new to the hospital, and no one knows that James Madison is her baby's father. She thinks about the woman in the room fighting for her life being the one who killed him. Raigen knows her. She knows her well. As a matter of fact, they've had drinks in Lug's apartment while the guys ran out to play ball on the court at times.

Raigen grabs the side of the sink because she feels like she's about to pass out, but she needs to keep going. Her love for Jimmy grows even stronger while her hatred for Lisa, the woman who she's had laughs with, grows intense. She exits the bathroom, and then, walks down the hall where the other nurses are gathering for their short meeting. She passes them all, and when she steps inside the hospital room, the last nurse leaves out, alerting her to the fact that doctors want the patient Lisa Caldwell to be monitored off the ventilator for right now and that she's a suicide risk. The door closes behind her. There lies Lisa.

Raigen walks over to her and carefully moves behind the curtain. Lisa is breathing, however, her eyes are closed. The oxygen mask is on her, and the percentage of oxygen going to her lungs reads at ninety-eight percent. Without one word to go along with the multitude of tears that are streaming down her face, Raigen removes the oxygen mask and covers Lisa's face and mouth with the palm of her hands. Then she waits. She watches as Lisa's chest moves up and down until it moves up and down no more. Then, she removes her hand from Lisa's face, and walks out of the hospital room, passing the huddle of nurses.

"Raigen, Raigen," the head nurse calls as Raigen passes by. "You can't leave…get back here now!"

Raigen continues to walk with her sights set on nothing in particular as tears swarm her cheeks. The only thing she imagines is her baby's father standing in front of her with his arms wide open. The police officer assigned to Lisa's room gets up when he hears another nurse yell what has happened. He runs to grab Raigen, who when she hears his footsteps, turns to face them all and plunges a needle into her neck while rubbing her three month pregnant stomach. She then falls to the floor.

Chapter Sins

I watch the cell door close every day. The only glimpse of daylight or nightfall comes through a small window above my bed. Most of the time, I just sit here on my bed unless they take me outside because I have a hard time walking and even talking on the left side of my body.

A number identifies me, and the only people who come and see me are Lug and my dad. Ma won't come because the last couple of times, she broke down and cried. She probably doesn't cry at the fact that I'm in prison now. Her sadness probably derives from how I look. The side of my face drags down with no muscle tone, and my eye, the same one that Robert hit before I killed him, is forever shut. I look crazy, and by the things I've done, I appear crazier. But so what if they think I'm crazy. I'm the only one who knows the truth.

I'm perfectly sane. For the most part, I'd kill them all again. Father, please, forgive me for my sins.

THE END

More Akirim Press Books

Books by Mirika Mayo Cornelius

Secret

Colored Lily: Poppa Took My Innocence

Paton

Ain't Quite What I Thought

Ain't Quite What I Thought 2

Inside the Gates of Doons

Sunny Sides of My Shade

Murders at Gabriel's Trails: The Complete 5 Part Series plus bonus Sins of Bain

Books by Rod Cornelius

Diggin' Gold

The Trusted

Single Again

Ghetto Eyes

The Best Kept Secrets

Ugly

Books by Cyan Deane

Dead Man's Mayhem

Execution's Karma

Preview **Murders at Gabriel's Trials: The Complete 5 Part Series plus bonus Sins of Bain** by Mirika Mayo Cornelius

Alexis spots Bain walking casually down the trail with his confident swag and cell phone to his ear. Whoever he was talking to, Alexis doesn't care. For the most part, she's just ecstatic to see that he is coming up the trail to meet her like her knight in shining armor. She trusts him so much until she feels like absolutely nothing can hurt her in the world, including in Gabriel's Trails. Besides that, Bain is well known for his handsomely strong stature and no hesitations when it comes to taking care of any trouble that comes his way. He's never killed anyone, however, but after he's finished dealing with anyone who crosses him, the word is that the victim of his anger wishes Bain had taken his life.

Bain is about six feet two in height, medium build but built into a brown skinned body that any woman would love, including young girl. He has a youthfulness about him that appeals to all the women because although he is all about no nonsense when it comes to what belongs to him, he's also tender and respectful and can make any woman blush, let alone a teenager. It is Alexis that has his heart though, and most ladies know this.

He's finally within arms' reach of Alexis and pauses before reaching out to embrace her. "Why did you walk this far up, Lex? You know I don't let you walk this far up the trail…"

"I'm a big girl, babe," she responds, tip toeing to plant him a kiss on the lips while he stands there and takes it all in, rubbing the small of her back like he wants to

247

undress her on the spot. The trail is lined by trees on both sides, and as Bain pulls back from the kiss, he gently turns her backwards so that she can see why coming this far into Gabriel's Trails is dangerous.

"Do you see the main road anymore, Lex?"

"No, Bain," she drags.

"Nothing but a trail that ends, curving back into where you came from. Nobody can see you anymore, Lex. At that point," he explains, pointing to a boulder that's painted red on the side of the trail, "Coming in here beyond that rock this far up means that you're on your own." He turns her back around so that he can look her in the eyes. "I don't ever want you to be on your own, Lex."

"Like I said, I got me."

Preview **SECRET** by Mirika Mayo Cornelius

"I told you your aunt is resting, didn't I?"

I reach my leg back and kick him in his mouth. He yanks his head back and stares at me like he's gonna kill me, so I kick him again with both of my legs swinging like a wild bat. He jumps on top of me holding my right leg with his hand and ducking away from my other leg while its kicking. He starts to unbuckle his pants with his other hand.

"Yeah, it's present time now. You done asked for it. I heard about your momma. A nice piece of work there."

He rips off my pajamas after he gets his pants down. My heart fills up with scary feelings when I just now figure out why my Aunt May said what she told me all the time. Where's Aunt Janie?

"Aunt Janie! Your friend is in my room! He's not supposed to be in here, Aunt Janie!" I yell the loudest I can yell.

Sam reaches back with his right hand and hits me on the side of my stomach. I curl up in a ball.

"Guess what, Secret. She ain't coming so ain't no use in you calling for her. You act like I'm about to hurt you. I wouldn't have hit you like that if you didn't try to wake up your aunt, so I'm sorry. Now hold still."

He feels up my back with his naked hand. My stomach is aching. He keeps acting like he ain't gonna do nothing to me, but this don't feel right. I keep thinking about Aunt May while his hand is going up my leg. I feel something wet on my leg, too. I yank away, but he jerks me in front of him. Jesus, please, help me, Lord. Tears are falling every which way down my face, but then I see it. I fell asleep with my pencil beside me in my bed. It's halfway covered up with my sheets.

"Touch it."

I look back at him, and he closes his eyes.

"Look down and touch it."

That's when I look down and see what he's talking about. I panic.

"Get off of me! No! I'm not touching that thing-ever! What is that? Aunt Janie, please!" I reach for the pencil real fast, but I don't know what to do with it yet. My hand grips the pencil like somebody else got it for me. My other hand grabs that long, ugly thing, and my hand, with the pencil in it, reaches all the way back and stabs that big, ugly thing right in the center.

He lets out the loudest holler I ever heard from a man in my life, and his eyes fly open. I jump up off the bed, and run towards the other end of my room. I look back at his ugly thing and see that the pencil is still stuck in there while he's tumbling around on the floor. His hands are around it, but he ain't pulling it out. It's hurtin' him so bad that I pick up my lamp so that I can aim for his head so I can bang some more pain into him. He justa hollering. Betcha he won't come in my room no more.

Preview **Diggin' Gold** by Rod Cornelius

She wanted him just as bad as he wanted her, but just not bad enough to get it on in the car. She also realized that another round with Trent meant another day of lying to Jimmy, but what he doesn't know wouldn't hurt him, she thought. Besides, she was trying to come up and Jimmy's stock was falling fast. Trent had tangible assets, and she was almost ready to go all in.

"I told you earlier that I had a lack of patience for you. Now how about let's get up out of this ride and take a no-holds barred tour of my humble abode. There won't be a piece of furniture off limits. I promise," he said as he continued feasting on her neck.

She observed his house again, "I don't know if you got a back strong enough for the kind of tour that you're talking about. Your place looks like it has a lot of ground to cover. It could take the whole night to get it all."

He pulled up and backed away from her. "There's only one way to find out."

"Then why are we still in your Jag?"

He backed away further with a smile as she smiled right back at him. "Baby, it ain't nothing but a word."

"Then what are you waiting on?"

"Shiiiiiit!" he said. She finally told him what his ears had been waiting all night to hear. The green light was lit. He knew he could have pretty much any woman he set his sights on but Kizzy carried an extra spiff. Not only was she sexy and a freak in between the sheets, but she was

Jimmy's lady. She was the last thing he could take from Jimmy and that was worth more than its weight in gold.

He quickly hopped out of the automobile and danced around the vehicle to open her door. He grabbed her hand to assist her on her exodus. He shut the door, not releasing her hand as they made their way to his front door.

As she stood behind him, she looked up and admired the huge brick home. She had never been in a house as big as his, and she couldn't wait to serenade it with him. "This really is a nice place, Trent. I could see you making me some pancakes in bed here," she joked.

"Oh we 'bout to make something, but it's not going to pancakes, that's for sure." He pulled her into the dark house and slammed the door shut. Then he pulled her into him and gave her a passionate kiss.

"So I guess you mean business," she said as she pulled away from his lips and rested her arms around his neck.

"Do I?" he smiled. He placed both hands on her rump and gripped it tightly, pulling her up off of the floor as she wrapped her legs around his waist. As his tongue ran its slow, slippery course up and down her neck, he walked her through the dark living space and carried her to the leather couch. He laid her down and his tongue twirled around her bosom as his hands made their way down her legs as he began to inch her dress upwards.

Preview **Dead Man's Mayhem** by Cyan Deane

What the hell was that? If they don't get their little southern asses out of my viewing! Rest in peace? Mary made my life a living, breathing, stinking hell, and she has her sweaty panties coming in here trying to start some real shit while I'm still trying to wake myself up from this doomsday nightmare.

Mary – she's the lady that built the straw house that I wanted to crap on each and everyday to make that thing fall down right on top of her ass. When I would walk into her bar, for some reason or another, she would always be there. What owner is always at their establishment? That's the purpose of hiring people to work for you while you sit your ass at home and play golf in the middle of lunch time traffic so everyone can see what a grand life you have. She would make her baggy eyeballs twitch at me, and she's only forty one years old, looking and sounding like a grandma of eight hell raisers.

Truth be told, Mary would constantly talk shit, but it was shit that I could never hear. Call me paranoid, but she was ten words from getting popped in her mouth the day I supposedly went cold. I still don't even know who knocked me over my damn head in her nasty ass bar, but I swear it was probably her ass that set me up. She hated me, and I could tell. Her raggedy bar wasn't even that good for anything, but I was determined to go inside each and every week to make her life-long dream of store ownership reek of irritation with my presence.

I'd come to find out that I dated Mary's second cousin, Barbara Sue, back in the day for like three minutes tops, and Barbara Sue had gone and told her whole felon ass family that I was the one who broke her heart into

253

pieces. First off, what they didn't know was that I would have never dated anyone seriously named Barbara Sue. Let's get that out there right now. Secondly, all I did was kiss her after talking on the phone with her for about one week.

When I met up with her, Barbara Sue wasn't really my type, but hell, the date was still on. We went to see a movie, parked it at the park, kissed and I took her snaggle toothed mouth home. It's true I never called again, but it was a damn shame how she ran my name in the mud about it.

Preview **Single Again** by Rod Cornelius

"Hey, do you have a name?" She didn't answer. She blatantly ignored me, just like she did when I first approached her in the club. Now see, it's things like that, that makes a man think with his brain and not his jimmy all of the time. But then I took another glance at her body and quickly realized how much more powerful a man's jimmy is than his brain. As a matter of fact, it is his brain. Besides, this chick was a perfect ten. A ten, then some. And those are just too hard to come by at times.

Her directions led me straight to a two-story brick house smack-dab in the middle of Brenton Avenue. "Keys," she chillingly requested. A brief thought of being stranded in the middle of nowhere swiftly raced through my mind. I gave her the keys. "Come on," she said. Thank you, Jesus. I couldn't bare the thought of walking all the way back to that club and trying to quickly compose a lie to Rex as to why I was perspiring so badly.

I jumped out of the car and shadowed her tracks like a starving dog sniffing for a meaty bone. She opened the door to the house and flicked on the lights beside the entrance. As I stepped into her crib, I began to instantly think that this experience had to be some kind of cruel joke sponsored by my subconscious and somehow, I was sleeping and couldn't wake up. And the way it was beginning to feel, this was gonna be a wet one.

She glanced back at me, "Close the door." I shut the door and followed her up the stairs. The house really didn't have much in it. In fact, it looked unlived in altogether. The walls were neatly entangled with an assortment of oil paintings but not much furniture consumed the home. Nonetheless, my primary concern rested on just one piece of furniture in particular - the bed! We walked into what had to have been the master bedroom. It was humongous. An exquisite Persian rug laced the floor. There was a huge floor-length window open, and the nightly breeze blew her finely-silk draperies into the room. Most significantly of all, she had this massive king-sized bed in the center of the room.

I looked around, not trying to seem overly-amazed. "So this is yours?"

"Nope!" she said as she walked alongside her bed, slowly sliding her fingers across the satin sheets.

Damn! I knew she had to have a man, somewhere.

"Well, it is for now. My agency is leasing this place for me until I find some place to live down here," she said.

"Oh," I said relieved that there was no sign of any manly presence in her life so far. "All this for you, huh?"

She grinned. "Yeap."

I walked over to the window and gazed down at the dimly lit street. I didn't want to seem too anxious for what she had to offer. "Nice view."

"I'll say," she replied.

I could almost feel her eyes cutting through my back. I turned around, thinking maybe I could slip a little bit of my own arrogance in there. "I was referring to the street."

"I was, too. What else would I be referring to?"

Ooh, low blow, and can't say that I didn't deserve it. As she took a seat on the bed, I just stared at her, not having a clue to where things were headed. But if I knew anything, I definitely had to have them go the direction I wanted them to.

"So," I took a deep breath. "Why did you bring me here?"

"Why did you come?" she quickly combated.

"What? You grabbed my hand and led the way."

"You're a grown man. I'm quite sure you could've stopped me."

Preview **Inside the Gates of Doons** by Mirika Mayo Cornelius

"Levi, we can't remove the knife man because it's gonna make another cut that might kill him," he stresses, attempting to remain calm while the gun is on his face, but calmness is such a fabrication because his lips are curled and his teeth are grinding up against one another as he speaks. "We gotta get him to the hospital just like he is and fast, but we gotta move. Taking the knife out is gonna make things worse. Trust me, man. I know." Roscoe then takes a deep breath, and speaks slower, enunciating every word from his mouth. His head is tilted, and only his eyes cut to the side to zoom in on Levi's finger on the trigger. "Now take the mother fuckin' gun from my face, Levi, if you're not gonna blow a hole in my head. Then you can think about how you're gonna move this man your damn self."

Maria is still screaming at an unbearably high pitch and shaking so badly that she can barely stand up. Séa covers her mouth in horror at the sight of Pierre in convulsions while blood seeps from his mouth. Then she spins around to face the woods, panicked by the plain facts -there's a killer among them, and he just tried to stab Pierre to death.

"Pick him up," Séa quietly states, and as she continues to strain her eyes to see further into the woods, she elevates her voice. "Pick him up, now! We gotta get outta here," she screams at Levi as he backs away from Roscoe's face with the gun. "Hurry!" She glares at Levi like she wants to shoot everyone if they don't make the right moves, and then she snatches the gun from his hand. "Gimme the gun, Levi. Give me the fuckin' gun, dammit!"

257

She quickly points the gun toward the woods, ready to fire at the first human moving that she doesn't recognize. Her heart beats rapidly through her chest, almost to the point of feeling like it will explode. Séa's a small young lady, but she's ready to defend herself at all costs. If anyone will shoot to kill, Levi knows that it's her, therefore, he plays the odds that she will more than likely hit the necessary target while he does something he has no choice but to do – relieve himself of the firearm and help Roscoe pick up a weak and bleeding to death Pierre off the muddy ground.

Preview **Ain't Quite What I Thought!** by Mirika Mayo Cornelius

I just stood there thinking, this nut has the key to my place and a bloody knife in my drawer. Immediately, I plopped down on my sofa and rocked back and forth, watching my reflection in the blank television screen. The whole reflection looked like a scary movie, circling around me at high speed.

"I'm gonna die if I leave this fool," I stated quietly. He already had me talking to myself and picking at my fingernails, ripping them apart. That's what I did when I got nervous. My fingernails would start off hot and sexy but then run into busted and disgusted really fast.

There was a Kleenex hanging from the box on the coffee table, so I wiped my neck. His blood got all over it. I bet Andre' had a criminal record a mile long that included strangulation and attempted murder. Before I'd even thought about that notion fully, I'd already turned on my laptop to do research. But then, I thought about Capital City. No, he had to be clean to run a place like Capital City, but it could be that he never got caught.

Panic struck as I thought about being the unsolved mystery that my mom and dad would have to watch on television because I didn't tell a soul who I was sleeping around with. That fact alone prompted me to go back up to that hospital to get words from Tina's mouth herself, even confess that I was sleeping with her husband if I had to do so. That way, I could get her angry enough to turn him in. He would be arrested, and that would leave me in the clear and safer than ever.

Needing to know more about Tina's situation consumed me like the oxygen I breathed, and I just had to know for a fact for my own emotional stability what happened fist by fist, including how possibly sick her

husband actually was. It would be my worst nightmare if
I'd messed around and sexed up a psycho.

www.ingramcontent.com/pod-product-compliance
Lightning Source LLC
Chambersburg PA
CBHW060312260626
47160CB00007B/2575